A Trail So Lonesome

WAGON TRAIN MATCHES
BOOK ONE

LACY WILLIAMS

One

IT WAS CROWDED and overwarm in the dance hall in Independence, Missouri, when Evangeline stepped inside.

But tonight there was no dancing, no music. The cavernous room was packed with bodies. Many of them unwashed, judging by the overwhelming scents that attacked her nose.

Several heads turned in her direction, eyes fixed on her, and she felt a tremble of nervousness.

Every person in this room was just like her. At least that's what she told herself.

This meeting was for travelers who had paid and been approved to travel on Hollis Tremblay's wagon train, leaving Independence tomorrow morning.

And Evangeline was going with them. Starting a new life.

"Sissy?"

Evangeline looked down into the face of the young girl clinging to her hand. Worried brown eyes looked up at her. Sara clutched a faded rag doll in her other hand, while Evangeline clutched a thick tome to her midsection.

Evangeline squeezed Sara's hand in reassurance. She

1

wasn't used to being in this press of bodies. Neither was Evangeline, but they'd make do. They had to.

"Our seats are right over there," she murmured with a nod forward and to the left, right in the middle of the room. Near the front, so they could see. The wooden chairs *had* been theirs when they'd left. Evangeline preferred to be punctual and had, in fact, been a half-hour early for this meeting. She and Sara had been nearly alone in the dance hall. Everything had been going just as Evangeline planned.

Until Sara had whispered that she needed the washroom.

After a trek back to their hotel, they'd returned minutes late—though the meeting didn't seem to have started—to find the dance hall packed.

Families of all shapes and sizes filled the room. A mother bent over several young children clustered at her feet, scolding them. A father stood against the wall, his arms folded. Two teenaged boys stood in an identical stance and the uncanny resemblance to the man so obviously their father made Evangeline want to smile. Rough-looking men were scattered among the crowd, too. One man with dark hair and an unkempt beard let his eyes linger on Evangeline for far too long as she scooted past him. She averted her eyes quickly but felt his unsavory gaze linger.

When she and Sara reached the seats they'd vacated minutes ago, they found them occupied. There had been no one around to ask to save her seat when she'd left for Sara's sake. What now?

A shrill whistle rang out over the noise of the crowd. "Good evening," a deep male voice followed.

The murmur of voices faded. Some people hissed, "Shh!"

Heat rushed into Evangeline's cheeks as she realized she had no seat, and she was awkwardly blocking several folks from being able to see the man who was speaking. She'd considered leaving her book on the chair, but it was too valuable to be left behind.

Now she tugged Sara by the hand as she hurried toward

the back of the hall, embarrassed as she felt the gazes of nearly everyone she passed. Several people were standing at the back of the room. She would have to do that, too.

Emotion knotted in her throat. She'd wanted—she'd *planned*—to be closer. What if she missed something important because she couldn't hear?

Her gaze caught on a woman who must be only a little older than Evangeline's twenty years. She sat on the second row from the back wall. She nudged the man beside her—her husband?—who scowled at her. The woman nodded to Evangeline, still side-stepping toward the back, and whispered something to him.

He looked up, his blue eyes locking on Evangeline. She felt his gaze almost like a touch and nearly stepped on the foot of the man right in front of her who had scooted his chair into the rough aisle, forcing Evangeline to step around him.

The blue-eyed man's scowl grew bigger. He said something to the woman and abruptly stood up.

Evangeline was close now. Before she could look away, he nodded to the empty seat and strode to the back of the room.

"...wagons packed."

Grateful and embarrassed at the same time, Evangeline slipped into the seat. She placed her book at her feet and pulled Sara onto her lap.

"Thank you," she whispered to her neighbor.

The woman gave her a sunny smile. "Certainly."

"You've been given a list of required food items," the wagon master said. "I've already inspected some of your wagons to see that your supplies are ready."

Evangeline had checked and double-checked the supplies in the wagon. She knew they'd purchased and packed everything on the wagon master's list, but her hands itched to check the list folded inside her book at her feet. She kept her arms loosely around Sara. She could re-check in a moment. No need to jostle the girl when they'd just gotten settled.

Father was supposed to have attended this meeting with

her, but he'd received a wire at their hotel and waved her on, declaring that he had to send an answer to his business partner back in Boston. Mrs. Fletcher, their long-time cook had opted to stay at the hotel. They were a long way from home. Everything was different. Evangeline was trying to make the best of things, but Mrs. Fletcher had been quietly complaining since they'd boarded the westbound train.

The friendly woman beside Evangeline leaned over to say something to the strapping man beside her. He patted her knee, something affectionate in the gesture. Was this her husband? Then who was the first man?

Evangeline couldn't help herself. She looked over her shoulder. The man who'd given up his seat wore a faded blue-and-white checked shirt over dark trousers. His dark brown hair was a little too long, as if he hadn't bothered to cut it. He stood with his arms loosely at his sides, but there was a leashed power about him.

His gaze flicked from the speaker to collide with hers. He glared at her, and it was so startling that she quickly turned back to face the front.

She couldn't help the tremble that went through her. Sara didn't register it as she fiddled with her doll.

The woman at her side noticed. "You all right?" she whispered.

"Fine," Evangeline whispered back. "But I don't think your husband is happy about me taking his seat."

The woman glanced over her shoulder. Evangeline couldn't read the face she made. She quickly turned back. "That's my brother. Leo. Don't mind him. That expression is near permanent. I'm Alice."

Leo. It was a name for an artist or poet, but he didn't look like either one. His muscular build was better suited for outdoor work.

"We'll be pulling out as soon as it's light," Hollis Tremblay said. The man was tall and broad, dressed in a pale blue shirt and fawn pants that contrasted with his dark brown skin. The first time Evangeline had met him, she'd felt a sense of peace at his steady confidence. This was his fourth trip across the country leading a wagon train. He was experienced and had a no-nonsense manner that she appreciated. "There are two other large groups leaving town, and we want to be the first on the trail."

That made sense. She'd studied every guidebook she could get her hands on—three of them—and understood that grass for the oxen could become scarce quickly.

"I'll ask one man from each family to stay behind after we're done here tonight. I've split the wagon train into three groups. We'll call each group a company for the duration of our travels. Each company will elect a group of leaders and one captain. We'll handle that and I'll give some final instructions."

The men.

Evangeline's face flushed. She'd thought Father would be here by now. Had his business tied him up? Or had he simply elected not to come, knowing she'd bring him whatever information was shared?

Now their family would miss its chance to have a vote for the captain of their company. What if someone unsavory—like the man who'd ogled her—became the leader of their group? What if something important was discussed and neither she nor Father knew about it?

This wouldn't do at all.

* * *

Leo Spencer was cataloging the tasks he needed to complete tonight as the wagon master spoke. Waterproof the seals on the wagon bed. Re-pack the dry goods they'd purchased late this afternoon.

Stop watching the woman.

He had noticed the dark-haired beauty as she had tried to find a seat in the packed dance hall. How could he not? The way her hair was pulled back from her face showed off her delicate features to their advantage. And that gown... it was too fancy to be called a dress. Completely impractical and wouldn't last a day on the trail. But it sure was nice to look at, especially on a figure like hers.

He'd noticed the little girl, too. Of course a fine woman like that was married. But where was her husband? Why hadn't he been at her side, scouted out seats for the little family?

He forced his mind from her, tried to pay attention to Hollis as he addressed the crowd. Leo had one mission, and he wouldn't fail: get his family to Oregon, get them settled.

Only then could he go after his own adventure. Maybe he'd join up with a railroad crew. He'd read newspaper accounts of the money they were offering for line workers. He was a hard worker. He could save enough to buy a ticket to Europe. Travel and see the world.

A man standing near the door on the opposite side of the dance hall distracted him from his musings.

His half brothers, Owen and August Mason, standing side by side.

What were they doing here? Checking up on Leo?

Distaste curled in his stomach. He must've made some noise, or maybe she just sensed his flare of anger; either way, his sister turned to look over her shoulder.

He nodded to Owen.

"We'll give the women and children five minutes to clear out." Hollis dismissed the meeting and folks began standing up, spilling into the spaces between the chairs.

A mother with her wailing baby stepped in front of Leo. He looked over her head. Owen was still there, holding up the wall with his shoulder as if he hadn't a care in the world. Seemed about right. Leo had inherited them all.

He started toward his half brother, the crowd preventing him from moving very fast. The young woman who'd taken his seat had already slipped away. No, there she was. Speaking animatedly to the wagon master, holding the little girl's hand. She still had what looked like a heavy tome in her opposite hand. Who brought a big book like that to a meeting?

His mind snapped back to Owen.

"Don't do anything stupid." Alice was right on his heels.

"Listen to Mother Hen," came his brother Collin's voice from right behind her.

It warmed him to know that his true family was right there to support him. Except— "Where's Coop?" he demanded.

Collin's twin had been in attendance. He'd sat next to Collin as the meeting started, looking bored to death. He must've slipped away when the meeting had been dismissed.

Collin sighed slightly as he must've come to the same realization.

Leo changed course, heading back the way he'd come. He scanned the room but couldn't see his brother in the melee. Frustration made him want to howl, but he didn't dare release the emotion. He never did.

Coop attracted trouble like metal shavings to a magnet. And there was plenty of it to be found here in Independence.

"Leo, you've got to stay for the meeting." Alice's reminder stilled his feet, but his mind was already counting the number of saloons he'd seen along the street. Coop had given his promise back in New Jersey. But after years of breaking his word, it didn't hold much.

"We'll find him," Collin said.

"Maybe he went back to the wagon." Even Alice didn't sound hopeful.

Leo gritted his teeth. He didn't have any choice. Hollis had said each head of household needed to attend the meeting. But Coop could stir up an awful lot of trouble, real quick. What if Alice and Collin couldn't find him?

"Something wrong?" The drawled question came in a voice that took Leo right back to his childhood. Why did Owen and August have to sound just like Leo's father?

Leo nodded to Alice and Collin, who disappeared into the crowd. Alice threw one look over her shoulder. Probably worried Leo was going to lose his temper.

It was a near thing, but he managed to face his half brother. "None of your concern. What're you doing here?"

Owen didn't just sound like Leo's father. He shared the same brown hair, same blue eyes, same hawk nose Leo saw every morning in the looking glass while he used his razor.

Seeing Owen now felt almost exactly like the invisible punch to the gut he'd received when Owen and August had shown up on his doorstep back in New Jersey. A sucker punch, one he hadn't known to anticipate.

Owen seemed unruffled. "Same as you," he answered Leo's question.

No. "You're not joining up with this wagon train."

Owen's eyes narrowed slightly at the command in Leo's voice. "'Fraid so. August and I mean to go back to California. That way, we'll be here when you and Alice need help."

"We won't need your help," Leo burst out.

The wagon master called everyone left in the room to huddle up closer to the center of the expansive space.

Owen bared his teeth in a smile and nodded for Leo to move ahead of him between the now-empty chairs. "You and Alice and those boys have no idea how to survive an arduous journey like this."

Leo shook his head. A months-long trip through the wilderness would be tough, but he'd never accept help from Owen or August. They were a reminder of the life his father had chosen—and the life he'd walked away from. One he'd started with Leo and Alice's mother and then abandoned.

Bitterness rose in his throat to choke him. This wasn't the time for it, though. He joined the circle of twenty or so men standing around Hollis, doing his level best to ignore the man on his heels.

A gray-haired man pointed to the young woman Leo had

given up his seat for, addressing the wagon master. "What's she doing here? You said men only."

The young woman stood her ground, her chin at a stubborn angle. "My father wasn't feeling well tonight. I'm here in his stead."

Father. Not husband.

The older man continued to grumble, but it was Owen who called out, "Let her stay. She looks intelligent enough to me."

The gray-haired man shot Owen a look, but it was the appreciative way the young woman glanced at him that made Leo's stomach curdle.

"This isn't a democracy," Hollis said. He sounded unruffled and completely in charge. "What I say goes. We'll be on the trail together for five months, give or take. If you question my orders while we're out there, you and your family could end up dead."

When they'd arrived in Independence, Leo had discovered there were many companies taking travelers across the country to Oregon and California. When he'd asked the locals, everyone had sung Hollis Tremblay's praises. He was the most experienced wagon master on the trail. And he sounded it.

The men shuffled their feet, now looking uncomfortable. Leo watched the young woman. She wore a serious expression and didn't seem like some fainting miss, even though she wore that fancy dress. The little girl on her lap didn't make a peep, vacillating between looking around with wide eyes and playing silently with her dolly in her lap.

"You already know my rules," Hollis said. "No thievin', no fighting. Take care of each other. But I can't watch over a hundred wagons and know what's going on at all times. That's part of the reason we're here tonight. You're my second company. Tonight we're gonna elect a committee. Three leaders who are responsible for the folks in your company. Out of those three men, you'll choose one captain.

After four weeks on the trail, we'll have another election. Choose a different captain."

Now the men looked around at each other, taking each other's measure.

"This is not a responsibility to take lightly," Hollis continued. "Or one to be abused."

Men started calling out the reasons they should be considered.

I've been the head of household for thirty years.

I'm good with a gun.

I can read a map.

Leo didn't need any extra responsibility. He was perfectly content to vote for someone else to take on that role.

Until Owen spoke up from beside him. "My brother and I traveled East from California this past winter. We know what kind of terrain to expect. What kind of animals we'll run across. What kind of men to avoid out there."

The same gray-haired man who'd spoken up earlier scowled. "I thought we were only allowed one representative per family."

He was glaring at the both of them, Leo realized belatedly.

"We aren't family," he said, jerking his thumb in Owen's direction. "And we're not traveling together."

A soft, disbelieving sound came from Owen, but Leo knew he was only playing it up for the crowd.

"That's not strictly true," Owen said. His lips had twisted in a smirk. "Leo's my half brother. But he's right that we're not traveling together. We've got two separate wagons."

Leo didn't want their family's dirty linen aired in this group—or at all—and he was aware of the woman watching them. Something galvanized him. He found himself saying, "I managed a team of ten at a New Jersey powder mill. I've dealt with plenty of conflict between my men, and I know how to get things done."

Owen grunted, and Leo had a moment of fear that the

other man would tell just how difficult a time Leo had keeping Coop in line.

But he remained silent.

Good. Owen might've seen Leo and his true family in a bad moment. But he didn't know Leo. And Leo didn't know him.

And he'd rather keep it that way.

"Let's put it to a vote," Hollis said.

Owen received three votes in a row and Leo felt his stomach turn. If Owen was voted captain, he and Alice and the twins might have to find another train to take the journey west.

But then Leo received two quick votes. None of the older men had received any.

When the young woman murmured Owen's name, Leo felt an irrational burst of frustration.

But when the votes had been tallied, Leo was the new captain, while Owen and a man named Clarence Turnbull were on the committee charged with keeping their company safe and organized.

Leo shook the hands of a few men nearby.

And then Owen extended his hand to Leo. "I'm glad to help—"

"I don't need your help," Leo said gruffly. He turned away without shaking Owen's hand.

And bumped into the young woman, who held the little girl in her arms. She looked like she was waiting to speak to Hollis, who was surrounded by men with questions.

Her eyes flashed to Leo's, and he felt that same moment of connection from earlier.

He didn't have time to feel anything other than worry about what kind of trouble Coop was stirring up right now.

He turned away and got out of there.

Two

"WHAT DO YOU MEAN, she's gone?" Evangeline whispered the words, standing outside the wagon with her father. "How could Mrs. Fletcher just abandon us?"

Sara was still asleep in the tiny pallet Evangeline had created inside the wagon, atop all their supplies. Sara had outgrown her crib months ago in their stately townhouse back in Boston. But this was different. Aware of how high the wagon bed was from the ground, Evangeline had put Sara's pallet in between two trunks, with a barrel of salt pork and a smaller one of sugar barricading the girl in.

How could Sara sleep through all this ruckus? The thin line of silver at the horizon was the only sign that the sun was rising, but the camp was bustling and had been for some time.

It didn't seem possible that so many of their neighbors were awake after the raucous celebrating that had gone on long into the night. But the teenaged boy two wagons away was working to get his oxen into their braces one-by-one. The family just beyond him were eating breakfast. If Evangeline remembered correctly, their name was Fairfax. An older brother barely twenty, a sister in the middle, and a teen brother. And their aunt. Evangeline's nose twitched at the scent of fried ham.

Her father was loading the last of the crates into the rear of the wagon and she realized their time was short, but she couldn't wrap her mind around what he'd just informed her. Their cook, a long-time employee and one of the only women in Evangeline's life after her mother had passed, would not accompany them to Oregon.

"She didn't want to go in the first place," Father said without looking up.

"I know that," Evangeline returned. "But she promised. You *paid* her." Her father had offered the cook an exorbitant amount to come West with them. For good reason. Evangeline had never learned to cook. Father and Mother had always employed a cook. And a housekeeper, a groom for their horses, two maids.

Evangeline had spent almost a year preparing for this trip. Reading about what to expect on the trail. Making lists and buying what they needed. Taking riding lessons. Sewing lessons.

But she hadn't spent any time in the kitchen because Mrs. Fletcher was coming with them.

"It's not too late to rethink this plan of yours."

She kept her smile in place, though Father's words stung. Actually, it was too late to change her mind. Almost four years too late.

We have to go. She didn't give voice to the words. *Sara needs Oregon.* There was no future for Sara back in Boston. No future for Evangeline, either, but she'd resigned herself to that a long time ago. She could change things for Sara.

Evangeline knew how to win her father. "Just think of all the timber in Oregon," she said. "Every family on this wagon train will want lumber to buy to make a new house. And you'll provide it for them. Along with the families that come next year, and the year after."

Her father was a shrewd businessman, and they both

knew she was right. Her father had built a series of successful mills under the tutelage of his father. The number of families traveling to Oregon with them was just the beginning. If there was a fortune to be made in Oregon, her father would be the one to make it.

He had listened to her opining about Oregon and the adventures—and the money—awaiting them on the other side of the country at the dinner table for nearly a week before she had won him over to the idea. She had been desperate, and he had finally seen the possibility.

He only glanced briefly at Evangeline. She ignored the pinch of hurt. "What will we eat for five months on the trail?"

"I'll cook."

It was still too dark to read her father's expression, but she could well imagine the skepticism she would see if there was light. Father didn't understand why this trip meant so much to her. "I'm certain I packed a cookbook."

He grunted. "Probably more than one," he muttered. "I'll start hitching up the oxen."

Evangeline had once been a spoiled girl, only worrying about the next fancy dress she would purchase for the next party. But that Evangeline had expired a long time ago. She straightened her shoulders and buoyed her resolve. How difficult could it be to cook over an open fire?

She took one last look at the skyline of Independence, now coming into relief as the first silver rays appeared on the horizon. She wouldn't let herself be frightened of this. There was no place for fear. Only courage.

"I don't suppose you've got an extra cord of rope." The oldest Fairfax brother was speaking to the neighbor between his wagon and Evangeline's.

She'd seen folks of all shapes and sizes in the meeting the other night. Stephen Fairfax seemed shy, had kept his head down during the brief introductions she and Father had made last night at camp.

She saw the slump of his shoulders and called out, "I have some extra rope."

She had packed the wagon meticulously, planned for a scenario just like this one. She and Father were perhaps at a disadvantage being from the city. But if she could help their neighbors and perhaps garner goodwill, surely it would make their journey easier at a later date.

She carefully stepped up into the wagon box, doing her best not to jostle the conveyance. She glanced to where Sara slept, though it was too dark inside the wagon to see anything other than a shadowy lump where she lay. Evangeline would have to wake the girl in a few minutes. They couldn't afford to stop for her to wash up as the wagons rolled out.

Evangeline reached into the small box that held the odds and ends she had packed as extras. She got back down from the wagon, waving the tied up rope like a prize.

"Thank you." His voice was fervent, though softer than she expected. She got her first good look at his face and realized he was younger than she'd thought. Much younger.

The smooth face with no hint of whiskers might belong to a 15-year-old. Surely she was mistaken. Maybe he was older but cursed by the fair skin he seemed to share with his sister. Some men didn't grow whiskers until an older age, right? Maybe he was even as old as seventeen. Not eighteen, surely?

He ducked his head and she realized she was staring. She cleared her throat. "You're welcome. I'm happy to help a neighbor."

He was gone before she could say anything else. She moved around to the back of the wagon, where the item she needed right now was packed away. She had to unlatch the tailgate and drag a box of ammunition out of the way before she found the crate she was looking for. It was packed with books, and she let her hand run over the spines of those at the top. She had packed and re-packed three crates just like this, her own personal library. She had filled every inch of space in each crate, re-arranging the books until not even a sheet of paper would fit between. She just knew there was a cookbook here.

"Pulling out in half an hour."

She nodded idly at the voice relaying the message, not looking up from what she was doing. Where was it?

"We won't wait if you're not ready. Half an hour." This time the starch in the male voice made her raise her head and look at him.

Leo Mason, the man who had been elected to captain for this first month of the journey. He had seemed resigned the other night; this morning he wore a stormy expression.

She abandoned her search for the cookbook and wiped her hand on her skirt before sticking it out and taking a few steps toward him. "I am Evangeline Murphy. My sister Sara is still sleeping, and my father is going to get the oxen. We'll be ready."

He stared at her hand doubtfully before he gave a limp handshake. "You have any problems, you can come to me."

"Or Owen. I remember."

His jaw tightened at the mention of his half brother. She had spent far too long last night remembering the tension between the two men during the meeting. Owen had seemed to take an ornery delight in announcing to the room that Leo was his half brother, as if anyone with eyes couldn't have seen the resemblance between them. She was an only child. When she had been young, she had often longed for a brother or sister. A companion to play with. Perhaps that was why she had spent so much time wondering at the broken relationship in a family of strangers.

"You'll want to keep the little one up in the wagon till we get clear of the creek." He pointed to a line of trees in the distance.

She didn't see a creek, but maybe he knew the landscape she didn't.

He started to walk off—without giving her a chance to

say anything else—but seemed to change his mind. "It's not too late for you to decide to stay."

She bristled. "What does that mean?"

"You don't look like you belong here."

How dare he? Her temper sparked hot prickles all up and down her arms. "I belong here as much as you or anyone else," she blurted.

He walked off, shaking his head.

And she was left trembling with anger.

The nerve of the man. He might not think Evangeline looked like a pioneer, but she had determination. If she had learned anything from her father in years of watching him do business, determination was all she needed.

* * *

Leo knocked his hat back on his head.

He should've let Owen win the vote for captain. It'd been a snap decision, but his stubborn pride hadn't wanted Owen in a position of authority over him. A stance he now regretted.

They hadn't even pulled out and he'd been called on to settle a dispute between two families. A dog had gotten loose of the rope it'd been tied to and eaten the neighbors' breakfast.

And he'd clearly offended Evangeline Murphy by his suggestion that she wasn't fit for this trip. Maybe it wasn't his business, but he didn't want to spend months alongside someone whose ignorance would cost them time and extra work. Those shoes! They were fit for a ballroom maybe, but he could almost guarantee she'd have blisters up and down her feet by lunchtime.

He wondered, not for the first time, if they'd made the right decision leaving New Jersey. It'd seemed the only decision in the face of the trouble Coop had stirred up. But this journey was a massive undertaking. He wouldn't have a moment's rest, not when he'd be watching over Alice and making sure Coop stayed in line.

Alice had barely stirred when he'd left the tent over an hour ago. Coop had been hungover and hadn't said a word to Leo, while Collin, always the peacemaker, had quietly gone about breaking camp. Why couldn't Coop be more like his twin?

The farther West they traveled, the better. There would be no saloons once they hit the plains. Leo had been careful to ensure no casks made it on board; not even for medicinal purposes.

He made his way through the wagons, the level of noise rising each moment. The folks traveling were excited; they hadn't had a taste of hardship yet. It'd be a quieter start tomorrow, he guessed.

A shrill whistle caught his attention. Hollis waved him over to a wagon outfitted and ready to go, the oxen in their traces. A man in fancy duds, dark pants and vest with a crisp white shirt that stood out in the breaking dawn, was with Hollis. Who was that?

Leo drew up short when he got within spitting distance. He knew that city slicker.

"I'm adding one more wagon to your company," Hollis said in lieu of a greeting. "Mr. Braddock joined up yesterday. I checked over his gear and everything seems to be in order."

Leo's eyes narrowed at the slightly younger man. He didn't move closer or attempt to shake the man's hand. What was this? A ploy? No hint of any lawmen Robert Braddock brought with him. Leo had believed they were free and clear of Braddock and his grandfather and the life they'd left behind in New Jersey.

Apparently not.

Hollis looked between the two men when silence reigned for too long. "Problem?"

Braddock stared at Leo. He could probably get Leo's

family kicked off the wagon train with a few words about Coop. But he only stared, his expression hard.

And Leo didn't want Hollis to know about Coop's trouble.

"You know how to drive those oxen?" Leo asked, forcing his tone into something polite.

The other man's jaw worked. "I'll make do."

"We're rolling out soon." Hollis strode away and left the two of them standing there, still staring.

"What do you want?" Maybe Leo shouldn't have growled the words, but seeing Braddock again had his heart pounding and his senses on high alert. Braddock had been the one to call for the police that terrible night at the powder mill. He'd been a part of the event that had set this whole thing in motion, sent Leo and his family far away from the only home they'd known.

"I'd like to speak to Alice," Braddock's words were guarded, his expression stoic.

No. The instant denial sprang to Leo's lips, but he stifled it as a memory of Alice, her face stained with soot and tears, held their friend Ellen in a crying heap. Ellen's husband had died in the explosion that night.

Braddock wasn't getting close to Alice or any of Leo's family.

"Whatever you've got to say, you can say it to me."

There was a crack in Braddock's calm expression. "I'll speak to Alice first."

The man's stubbornness only intensified Leo's resolve not to let him anywhere near his sister.

"If you came all this way for a chat, I'll have to ask you to move your wagon. We're getting ready to move."

Braddock's eyes sparked. "I aim to get to Oregon, same as you. Where's Alice?"

In the bustle of the morning, Leo hadn't noticed someone sidling up to him, but now a tall figure stepped beside him, facing Braddock.

Owen crossed his arms over his chest, looking menacing. "What's going on?"

Braddock's gaze moved between them. "Who're you?" he demanded.

"Who're you?" Owen returned. "If you're a part of this wagon train, you'd better mount up."

In the distance, a bugle sounded. A dog bayed, and from an even further distance, a weapon discharged.

Braddock eyed the two of them. Just when Leo thought he would keep arguing, he turned to boost himself into the seat of his wagon

Leo skirted Braddock's wagon. If they were pulling out, he wanted to be on horseback.

Unfortunately, Owen followed. Several wagons were rolling slowly forward, and Leo made sure to move quickly out of their way.

"I didn't need your help," he muttered. Owen already knew too much about what had transpired in New Jersey. He and August had walked into their lives at just the wrong time.

"Thanks for your help, brother," Owen mimed, as if Leo had said the words.

Leo's temper sparked. "We're not brothers," he burst out. He turned to face Owen squarely and his hand fisted at his side.

It was like looking at his father all over again, though his memories of the man were hazy. Maybe not memories at all.

"You don't want me in your life, but too bad. August and I *are* your family."

Leo shook his head.

"You're gonna need us before this journey is over." Owen made the words sound like a threat, one that Leo immediately wanted to refute.

Until he realized someone was shadowing them. His face flushed with heat as he turned to acknowledge the slight figure behind them.

Evangeline, and she looked as if she wished she was anywhere else.

"We'll finish this later," Owen muttered before he stalked off.

No, they wouldn't.

He worked to clear the traces of anger from his expression. "You need something?" Maybe he hadn't been able to eradicate every trace of frustration because she balked at his impatient tone.

She had something clutched to her chest and now brought it out to show it to him. It looked like some kind of journal. Even if he'd been able to read, he wouldn't have been able to make out the scrawled handwriting she showed him.

"I wanted to ask whether we'll be staying the night at Cow Hollow creek, or if we'll go five miles farther, to the meadow described in this guidebook."

That's what she wanted to know? Right now, while they were pulling out?

"We'll pass the night where Hollis tells us."

"I was just wondering, because the guidebooks say—"

He cut her off with a sharp wave of his hand through the air between them. "Ma'am, you'd do best right now to worry about your little sister. Make sure she's safe in the wagon. There's a lot of animals moving around, and if she were to get stepped on, it'd be bad."

Color rose in her cheeks. Her lips pinched, and he was sorry if he'd hurt her feelings, but he didn't have time for this right now.

He tipped his hat and turned away, heading straight for his wagon.

He needed to tell Coop to stay out of sight. If Braddock had come for some kind of retribution, his brother needed to watch out.

Three

TWO DAYS.

Coop couldn't keep his promise to stay out of trouble for two days.

Leo wheeled his horse, balancing on his right leg in the stirrup as the animal completed a neat turn and then sprung into a full-out gallop.

Leo was supposed to be driving the wagon this afternoon, but here he was riding herd on the twenty head Collin had insisted they needed for their future homestead. Leo had assigned Coop the task of pushing cattle today, mostly to keep him out of sight of Braddock. But apparently Coop couldn't be bothered to do his job.

At least, that's what Leo assumed. His brother had simply disappeared and left the cattle free to roam.

They'd taken their chance and scattered. It'd taken him almost an hour to round up eighteen out of the twenty. Lucky for him, the wagon train was settling in for the night so he wouldn't have to push the animals to catch up. While Leo had been out chasing heifers, Hollis had called a halt and the line of wagons had slowly been forming a large circle. Or rather, oval.

Hollis had warned Leo in private that it would take a week for most folks to get acclimated to this kind of travel. Today was only day two, and he'd already had to break up two arguments over a better spot to water oxen in the creek. Circling the wagons was meant to be a protective measure. Thank heavens they were still close to civilization because the scraggly egg-shape wouldn't protect much. The wagons needed to be closer together.

Maybe everyone just needed to get to know each other better. They were still strangers, after all.

Maybe some of them would turn back.

And that made him think of Miss High and Mighty Evangeline, with her maps and journals.

He realized he'd been curt with her yesterday morning when the wagons had been pulling out. When he'd stopped by her wagon last night to apologize, she'd accosted him with questions of why they'd stopped where they had, worries that the trail was already diverging from what was written in those books of hers, and thoughts on where they might cross the Platte.

The Platte.

The river was at least four hundred miles ahead of them. He'd been overwhelmed by her pointed questions and when she'd tried to shove a book under his nose, he'd managed to lose his cool again.

He should've just told her he couldn't read. She'd probably stop waving books in his face if he admitted to it.

But his pride wouldn't let him. She was pretty, and obviously educated, yet she was looking to him for answers.

And maybe he liked that a little too much.

He'd managed a team of ten men back at the powder mill. Four had operated the equipment and chemicals inside the mill while the others had jobs in the yard. He'd had a good relationship with his men. He didn't let authority go to his head or cloud his judgment. He was level-headed and even-tempered.

But there was something about Evangeline Murphy that got under his skin.

If he was smart, he'd forget all about her. And Coop.

He'd fill his belly and find his bedroll and start fresh tomorrow.

But Coop rode up unabashed and completely at ease as Leo was pushing the last pair of steers to join the herd.

"You put the family's livelihood at risk," Leo grated out by way of greeting.

Coop immediately bristled. "How's that?"

"What if a predator had attacked one of our cows while you were off gallivanting around?"

Coop snorted a laugh. "Do you see any wolves around here? Maybe a cougar hiding in that farmer's field? We're too close to the city to be in any danger."

That wasn't the point. "Where were you?"

Coop's eyes glinted. "Unless you got some new authority with that captaincy, I don't have to report my every move to you."

Leo felt suddenly exhausted. He didn't want to have this battle every single day for the next five months. Why did Coop have to be like this?

He tipped his hat back and rubbed his aching forehead. "Do you want Alice out here riding herd?"

Coop's eyes narrowed.

"Because that's what will happen if you don't do your part. Alice knows how important those cows are for when we get to Oregon."

Coop knew, too. They'd spent every penny of the inheritance from Leo's father to outfit the wagon and purchase those cows. They'd be able to file for a homestead when they got to Oregon, but it'd be coming on winter, and they'd be real short on supplies.

If they lost even one of the cows, it could mean trouble.

"You really want Alice out here on horseback?" Leo asked.

Coop scowled. Alice wasn't a strong rider. She'd fallen from a horse as a young girl and been frightened of the animals ever since.

The last thing their family needed was Alice getting herself killed because Coop wouldn't play nice.

"Alice is a big girl."

"Of course she is. But you're her brother. It's your job to protect her."

Coop's frown grew deeper. "I thought keeping us all in line was *your* job."

Leo wanted to put his brother in his place. When Leo had been fifteen and Coop twelve, it had been easy enough. He'd wallop his younger brother, and Coop always seemed to get the message.

But there were too many folks around for him to try it now.

Like the little girl and her mother who were walking back from the creek, a handful of yards in the distance. The wagons weren't that far either, with a couple of men ground-tying their horses or putting up tents. Plus, Coop had an inch on him and had been known to fight dirty before.

Coop seemed to know what Leo was thinking, or at least to take a good guess, because his smile widened even as his eyes narrowed.

"Get the cattle settled for the night," Leo ordered. "If something happens to them, you know who I'll be looking at first."

Leo wheeled his horse before Coop could respond. He kept a sharp eye out for Braddock but didn't see the man anywhere nearby this part of the circled wagons. Leo, on horseback, passed by the other man earlier in the day. Braddock had been struggling with the reins. His oxen didn't seem to want to follow his orders.

Served him right. Braddock was the grandson of a mill owner. He'd been born with a silver spoon in his smarmy mouth. Hadn't had to do a single day of real work in his life.

Leo walked his horse to where Alice and Collin had stopped the wagon for the night. Alice was working some magic with the cookpot, and Leo's stomach rumbled. Then his nose twitched as he recognized the scent of acrid smoke.

He reined in and dismounted, quickly moving to unsaddle the animal before anyone else in camp needed him.

His bedroll and some shuteye sounded better and better.

He caught movement from the corner of his eye and realized that Evangeline and her tiny sister were in front of the wagon right next to his.

Of course she was. Probably wanted to accost him with an armful of books and a hundred more questions.

Right now, she was fanning black smoke from the pot over her cookfire. She held a thick book, using her thumb and little finger to keep it propped open in her other hand. Was she really trying to read while she cooked? No wonder her food was burnt.

Leo focused back on the buckle beneath his fingertips before she looked up and saw him. He didn't have it in him to deal with Miss High and Mighty right now.

"Seems like you might should check on the little neighbor lady."

Leo bristled. Had Owen sought him out on purpose? Just to needle him?

He kept his eyes on his task. "Cooking supper isn't a captain's task."

Owen scoffed. "Maybe not, but doesn't the Good Book give some direction about being a good neighbor?"

Was his not-brother really going to preach to him? Leo was tired and hungry, and he'd dealt with one more petty squabble than he had patience for. He ignored Owen and removed the horse's saddle, tucking it underneath the wagon.

He thought he heard a soft sigh from the man, but it might've just been the wind in the tall prairie grass.

"If you won't ask her to eat with you, I will."

Leo continued to ignore his brother. He removed his

horse's bridle after slipping on a rope around its neck. He staked the horse on the other side of the wagon where it would have enough grass to graze on for the night.

Then he walked into the circle of light cast by the cook-fires and happened to catch Evangeline's gaze. Owen stood between them, his back to Leo. He was far enough away that Leo couldn't hear what he was saying.

Evangeline's gaze moved to Owen. She smiled at him.

And Leo turned away. Maybe if he'd been more friendly, she would've smiled like that at him.

Maybe he didn't want her to smile at him, not if she thought someone like Owen was worth smiling at.

* * *

Supper was ruined.

Evangeline kept stealing glances around the campsite to see who was watching her humiliation. No one appeared to have noticed, or at least they were all pretending everything was fine.

Until Owen Mason approached.

Maybe he wasn't coming to talk to her. She glanced away, her eyes landing on Leo striding between two wagons. He had put her off when she had tried to ask questions about the upcoming days of travel. He'd been impatient and short with her.

So of course he was also here to witness her humiliation. There was no way she and Father and Sara could eat the charred remains of the potatoes and chicken she had been trying to cook in the pot.

"Looks like you've had a mishap." Owen's gentle words drew her gaze back to him.

"There's no need to be gentlemanly about it. This is a complete disaster." Perhaps if she could make light of it she wouldn't burst into tears.

Father had already come to check on her once, stating

how hungry he was. That was before she had totally burned the meal. She could only imagine his frustration when he came back from watering the oxen to find no food at all.

He wouldn't say a thing, although that familiar muscle in his cheek would tick and his eyes would shutter.

But it would be the silent censure that would keep her awake tonight.

"Maybe it's your cookbook." Owen's smile was charming, but she had grown impervious to charming smiles after Jeremy.

She closed the book with a snap. "It's completely my fault. I—I'm not much of a cook, and I think trying to manage over an open fire did me in." She hadn't been able to find the outdoor cookbook she remembered packing. She had either misplaced it or overlooked it when she had gone through the crates of books. Or maybe Mrs. Fletcher had borrowed it and hadn't returned it before she had abandoned them.

"I'm pretty sure any of these ladies would be willing to give you cooking lessons." His arm moved in an expansive arc around the circle of wagons. "Folks are going to need to lean on each other. It's going to be a hard journey these next months. No shame in asking for help."

She felt the hot blush in her cheeks. She knew there was no shame in needing help. She just preferred to be the one giving it. She had donated her time to several charities back home. She enjoyed helping those in need.

But not knowing all the womanly skills that her neighbors seemed to have in spades humiliated her.

"August and I cooked up twice as much as we can eat. Why don't you and your family join us tonight?"

She tried to gauge his sincerity. Was he making a friendly overture? Or was he flirting? She was too desperate and hungry tonight to argue with herself about being careful.

"Sissy, I'm hungry," Sara whined.

Evangeline placed her hand on the tot's head.

Owen raised his brows, his expression friendly and open.

And there was Father coming around the wagon.

Evangeline loosened her tongue. "We'd love to join you."

Father must have been famished, because he didn't argue at all.

As Owen led them past the captain's wagon, he called out a hello to Alice, who was stirring her pot. Delicious smells emanated from inside it.

"You met Evangeline, Alice?" Owen said.

Evangeline's blush burned hotter.

"Yes, that night at the dance hall." Alice's eyes twinkled. Was she always so cheerful? How did she manage it? "How are you?"

"Fine," Evangeline choked out.

By the time they reached Owen's brother August, crouched near his cookpot on the other side of the captain's wagon, Owen was chatting easily with Father. His friendly manner made it easier on Evangeline, and she soon found herself with a tin plate of what August claimed was roasted rabbit.

"You should ask Alice for cooking lessons," Owen said, voice quiet. Father and August were conversing about tomorrow's trail.

"Maybe I will." But Evangeline's smiled slipped. Should she offer to pay Alice?

She'd been hungrier than she thought, her plate was almost empty when she noticed that Sara had abandoned her seat on a stump beside Father.

Her breath caught in her chest for a moment as she glanced around. There she was. But her relieved exhale was cut short when she realized Sara had sidled up to Leo, standing half-hidden in the shadows between the two wagons. He was still eating.

"Would you excuse me for a moment?" she asked Owen.

She left her empty plate on the tailgate of his wagon and scurried over to where the little girl now had the strapping man squatting at her level.

Sara was babbling. In her flustered state, Evangeline couldn't make out the words.

And then Leo took some thing out of his breast pocket behind his vest and showed it to the little girl. A feather.

"I found it under some trees today. I figured a big hawk must've been sitting on one of the branches waiting for a little critter to go by."

Evangeline stopped right behind Sara and placed her hand gently on the top of the girl's head.

Leo stayed in his crouch and looked up at her. For once, his face didn't seem to be creased with criticism and impatience. When he had been speaking to Sara, his voice had been warm and kind. There was something in his eyes now that made Evangeline's stomach tip.

"Your brother invited us to share a meal with him."

Some emotion flickered across his face before he carefully blanked it. "You'll want to watch yourself with Owen."

"Why? Is he a scoundrel?"

"I don't know him well enough to say such a thing. I don't know him at all."

How could that be? And yet, she could understand if there was a family break. She had one aunt back in Boston that her father hadn't spoken to in twenty years.

He must've seen the questions in her expression, but he was quick to shift his attention back to Sara, who was examining the feather from every angle.

"Your sister can keep that if she wants." He stood up and tipped his hat and strode outside of the circle of wagons and into the growing twilight. He hadn't smiled at Evangeline once.

He'd been kind with Sara.

Clearly, it was only Evangeline that he didn't like.

Four

LEO ROLLED out of his tent while it was still dark, battered by dreams of the explosion in those last moments before wakefulness. He could practically smell the bad powder, a little like strong vinegar. His ears echoed with screams of the two men who had been injured. They hadn't been a part of his team, but he'd known them for years.

He'd woken trembling, and not wanting to wake Alice, had slipped from the tent. It wasn't long until daybreak, but there was no use trying to sleep longer. Not for him. Not after that nightmare. Although even a few minutes more might've allowed him to wake feeling refreshed, instead of feeling as if every ounce of his body was dragging him down.

He needed his wits about him today. Last night, Hollis had informed him that the river crossing ahead was a flat, shallow crossing. But it was also the first one for folks. They would cross midmorning.

It was misty—a soft, persistent rain had fallen all night—and hard to get a sense of his surroundings. He wanted coffee. That would have to wait.

His sleep-addled brain circled back to another thorny issue.

He'd laid awake in his bedroll for far too long thinking about his neighbor.

Sure, she was beautiful to look at. Like an expensive porcelain doll in a shop window, something you weren't supposed to touch because you might get it dirty.

He had seen the way her gentle hand landed on Sara's head. When the young girl had looked up at her lovingly, he'd felt a pang of grief like he hadn't in a long time.

He'd been fourteen when ma had died, and it must've been years since the the last time she had touched him in such a gentle way.

He missed her.

And not just because of the responsibility that had been pressed on his shoulders when she died.

Alice was always one to give hugs or pat his arm. But that moment shared between the two sisters had somehow triggered an emotional reaction he hadn't expected.

His reaction to missing his ma had sent him out to check on the cows, where he'd found Coop inhaling the dinner Alice had brought him. Thankfully, his brother had seemed to understand the seriousness of Leo's warning from earlier.

When Leo had returned to the campsite, he'd found Evangeline and Owen talking near his half brother's campfire, each one seated on an overturned crate. Sara had been asleep on Evangeline's shoulder, and the two adults were so engrossed in conversation that they didn't even notice Leo sliding into his tent.

He had laid awake too long listening to the cadence of their voices before everything went quiet.

Owen had been smartly dressed the first time Leo had ever seen him. He'd delivered the news that he was Leo and Alice's brother, and he'd waved around the wad of cash he had brought, like Leo should be grateful to him.

Leo didn't want an inheritance from his late father. He didn't want anything from the man. His father had abandoned him and Alice when they had been infants.

As far as he was concerned, his brother and Miss High and Mighty deserved each other.

As he was tightening the cinch, ready to take his horse to the little tributary to water it, a frantic whisper came from the direction of the Murphy wagon.

"Sara!" The whispered call came again. Leo's feet carried him toward the wagon before he'd given a thought to going over there. Evangeline was crawling out of the tent next to her wagon. He couldn't make her features out in the dark. She startled when she saw him.

"What's wrong?" he asked.

"I woke up and needed to—"

"Take care of some personal business?" He supplied when she seemed agitated that she couldn't say what she meant.

"Sara was fast asleep. She didn't so much as twitch when I left the tent. But now she's gone."

"Maybe your father has her."

A loud snore emanated from inside the wagon, where James Murphy must have made his bed.

Evangeline was wringing her hands.

A little girl could get into a lot of trouble in a camp like this. He'd witnessed firsthand a toddler stepped on by one of the oxen—her foot broken badly. Surprisingly, Maddie Fairfax had helped doctor the little boy, though he might never walk right again.

"She can't have got far. Why don't you look around the wagons here while I make a circuit around camp." His horse was already saddled. It was the least he could do.

She gripped his hand tightly, and he was surprised by her strength and fervor. "Thank you." Her voice shook, and he had a sudden urge to pull her close, offer comfort.

It was so sudden and so startling that he stepped away instantly. What was he thinking?

"If we don't find her in the next few minutes, we'll wake up some folks and get them to help us. All right?" he asked.

She nodded, enough reassurance for him to mount up.

* * *

Evangeline choked back panic as Leo rode off. She circled Father's wagon to find the lantern and lit it with shaking hands.

Why would Sara wander off by herself in the dark? Was this God's punishment for Evangeline's sins? No. She had been forgiven, even if it was sometimes hard to accept it. Maybe Sara had needed to use the toilet. Maybe she had followed Evangeline, though that seemed unlikely. She would've encountered Sara on her way back to the tent.

She walked around their wagon and tent, calling out softly. Should she wake Father? She was afraid of receiving more silent censure. How could she have made a mistake like this? She should have woken the young girl and brought her along. Or waited until the sun was up, though her bladder had insisted she couldn't wait any longer.

Rain pattered on the canvas of the wagons and tents as she ranged farther and farther from their camp. People were stirring now, soft murmurs sounding inside some of the tents. Stephen Fairfax was trudging back toward the tents in the near darkness, still tugging his shirt into place.

He startled when he saw Evangeline, though she barely noticed.

"Have you seen Sara?" she called out in a trembling voice. "My little... sister? I thought she was asleep in the tent, but now she's gone."

The young man tilted his head so that most of his expression was hidden. "I haven't. But I can help look—for a bit. Want me to go back the way you've come?"

Tears stung behind Evangeline's nose. "Yes, thank you."

The young man passed her, headed back to camp.

Evangeline judged the distance she'd already come. She'd traversed halfway around the outer edge of their circled wagons. Could Sara really have come this far?

She could hear the creek burbling from here. Last night

she and Sara had walked down to the bank of the small tributary that fed into the river they'd cross today. They'd watched
as men and women brought their oxen and horses to the
water to drink.

Sara had tugged and pulled until Evangeline had given in
and guided her to a flat, sandy area where the water had
trickled so slowly it almost wasn't moving at all. She'd
removed Sara's shoes and stockings and allowed her to wade
in the water.

Sara had been ecstatic, shrieking with glee, bending to
splash water with her hands, picking up sticks and small rocks
to throw into the water.

Those happy moments from last night were overshad-
owed now by Sara's absence. Where was she?

A sudden, terrible thought hit. What if Sara had tried to
go back to the water?

The creek was on the other side of camp. Evangeline had
felt safe enough with the distance last night.

But now...

Fear set Evangeline's feet to running. Her chest tightened.
She couldn't catch her breath. Surely she was frightening
herself for no good reason.

Sara couldn't have come so far all alone in the dark?
Could she?

Rapid   hoofbeats   sounded   from   some   distance
behind her.

"Sara!" she called out as her feet touched the edge of the
rocky creek bank. Her voice seemed to be sucked away into
the shadowy morning gloom. This wasn't the shallow place
they'd played last night. The ground dropped away to a
deeper curve in the creek, dark water deeper than Sara was
tall.

The hoofbeats grew nearer, but in Evangeline's panic she
barely registered them.

"Sara!" she called again.

And there was Sara, several yards downstream, right at the

edge where the water met the bank, her white nightgown a beacon against the dark landscape.

"Sara! Don't move."

But Sara looked away from Evangeline, toward the water.

Evangeline ran.

As she watched in horror, the muddy bank shifted and crumpled beneath Sara's feet. Her little arms flailed, and then she plunged into the rolling waters.

Evangeline screamed her name.

Sara's head bobbed to the top of the water, but Evangeline could see it sweeping her downstream—toward Evangeline.

Only she didn't know how to swim. She'd never learned, hadn't even waded in last night with Sara.

But she reacted without thinking. She plunged into the water herself, the icy crush against her legs almost knocking her off her feet.

The swift current tossed Sara as if she were a rag doll, but it also dragged her toward Evangeline. All Evangeline had to do was catch her.

She lunged through the water. Her foot slipped, and she went under. Water went up her nose. She gagged, inhaling even more.

Still, she grabbed for Sara, even though the dark waters made it impossible to see. Where—?

Her hand encountered fabric. She gripped with all her strength and struggled to get her feet underneath her. She stood, gasping and spluttering, clutching Sara's nightgown in her fist.

She dragged the girl against her, got her arm around Sara's waist. She tucked Sara to her chest, legs still battered by the rushing waters.

Sara coughed and gasped for breath. Evangeline instinctively whacked her between her shoulder blades. Sara spewed water on Evangeline's shoulder and finally inhaled a full breath.

The current was still raging, trying to sweep Evangeline off her feet. One wrong step and she'd go under again. What if she couldn't hold on to Sara?

And then a massive brown horse emerged from the shadows, splashed into the water.

Leo!

He reached down. Evangeline raised her arm to meet his hand.

He swept her up, even as the waters pulled at her feet and sodden skirt. Cold air made her shiver as he settled her sideways across his lap, Sara sobbing against her shoulder.

Evangeline ran a shaking hand over the girl's hair, her shoulders. She put her mouth close to Sara's ear. "Mama's got you. It's all right now."

Evangeline snapped her mouth shut, realizing the truth had slipped out in this moment of fading terror.

Mama.

Had Leo heard?

His horse moved beneath them as he guided it farther upstream and then out of the water. His arm was strong and steady around her waist. For the first time since she realized Sara was missing, Evangeline drew a steady breath.

"She all right?" His voice was low and steady and made strange by the fact she could *feel* his words through the wall of his chest, where she leaned.

Sara still had her face buried in Evangeline's neck, but the strength of her sobs and the clutch of her arms was reassuring.

"I think so," Evangeline said. "She slipped off the bank—" Her voice caught as her mind replayed those terrifying moments. She couldn't look at Leo, afraid he'd heard the slip of her tongue.

His hand was wide and warm on the center of her back. "I saw. I saw you go in after her, too. It was a mighty brave thing you did for your sister."

Sister.

Relief overcame the tension gripping her. Maybe he hadn't heard her after all.

She finally looked away from the top of Sara's head. They were so close that there was nowhere to look but into Leo's face.

Her breath stalled in her chest.

The way he looked at her...

Gone was the critical expression he'd worn nearly every time their paths crossed. Now there was something intense in his eyes, something that made her stomach dip precipitously.

She swallowed hard, and his eyes seemed to darken.

She knew this feeling.

Attraction.

And he felt it, too.

The floating feeling inside her changed to trepidation, made her stomach clench.

She jerked her eyes away from his gaze, tipped her chin down. Made her voice cool, as she struggled for evenness. "Could you take us back to camp? I'm sure my father is worried."

A long moment passed before he cleared his throat. "Yeah."

She closed her eyes, pressed her cheek against the crown of Sara's head. She'd almost lost her, the precious girl for whom she'd given up everything.

Leo had rescued them both, and she'd sounded ungrateful. Maybe she could've climbed out of that creek on her own, but the strength of the current and Sara in her arms would have made it precarious. It could've ended badly—for both of them.

"Thank you for your help," she whispered.

"I would've done the same for anyone in our company." His voice was almost as cold as the wind biting her wet skin.

Five

"DO YOU SEE THIS RED BIRD?" Evangeline sat on an overturned crate with Sara on her knee and a thick book open in her lap.

Late afternoon sunlight slanted over the circled wagons. Hollis had called for an early stop today, promising that there was a long stretch ahead of them tomorrow. Thirty miles. Their longest day yet.

Evangeline was relieved to have a shorter day. After the early-morning disaster with Sara, she'd been thrown right into the day's work and hadn't had a moment to even breathe. Having an extra hour to themselves to rest, before supper preparations?

It felt like Heaven.

She tapped the hand-drawn picture on the page in front of them. "This is a cardinal. We saw him earlier when we passed by the woods."

Sara's chubby finger jabbed the page. She'd been quieter today, after the ordeal at the creek, and had taken a long afternoon nap.

Father rounded the wagon, holding a pair of his trousers. His eyes sought her out.

"Ripped a hole in these climbing down from the wagon. Do you think you can mend it?"

"Of course." She sounded more confident than she felt. During the winter months preparing for this trip, she'd sewn stitches in spare scraps of material. Her mending might not be pretty, but it would hold. She hoped.

He laid the pants over the side of the wagon. She'd get them later and do the mending.

But he didn't walk away immediately.

She glanced up at him, curious.

"Two families turned back today. The Smiths and Hybels. It's not too late to go back to Boston."

Not too late? They'd sold their home, and her father had bought out his silent investors. There was nothing left for them there.

Her stomach pinched. "I think we are doing all right," she said carefully. "A few more cooking lessons with Alice and I'll be a regular chef."

If she was still horrible, well... surely they could hire a cook once they got settled in Oregon.

Father opened his mouth and then closed it. Opened it again. Her father was a shrewd businessman, known for making and acting on quick decisions. What was he waffling about?

"We get much further west and it'll be harder to turn back."

"I don't want to turn back." Her voice had too much snap to it. She sucked in a breath and tried to form her lips into a smile. "Sara and I are quite enjoying our new adventures." That wasn't strictly true, not after this morning.

Father was frowning. Not directly at her, but with his face in profile she had a perfect view of the muscle jumping in his jaw.

She hadn't told him where she'd found Sara this morning, the near-drowning they'd both had. She'd only slipped into the tent, with Sara in tow, and gotten them both changed as quickly as possible.

Had Leo mentioned to him what had happened at the creek? Was he worried about the dangers of the trail? She couldn't think of another reason why he'd question her now. Not after the meticulous plans they'd made together.

Father's words had made her go tense. She forced herself to relax when Sara murmured, "This one?"

She pressed her cheek to Sara's head briefly. "That is a bluebird. Do you see its rusty feathers here?"

Before she looked up again, Father walked off without another word.

She wished they had the kind of relationship where she could've asked him what he was thinking, what he was worried about.

But they didn't.

That was the kind of relationship she'd had with her mother. But Mother had been gone since just before Evangeline's eighth birthday.

Father didn't know how many nights Evangeline had cried herself to sleep after Sara had been born—after overhearing a conversation between Mandy Nordstern and some other socialite friends that Evangeline couldn't even remember. It was Mandy who'd whispered behind her fan, "*Who'd ever want to marry Evangeline now? Or her illegitimate daughter, when she grows up! Their family money might make people smile to her face, but her father's all she'll have...*"

It'd been the first party Evangeline had attended after she'd given birth, and she'd snuck away without her former friend knowing she'd been overheard.

In that moment, everything had changed.

She didn't care about the slight to herself. After Jeremy, she didn't want to fall in love, make promises to someone who wouldn't keep them in return.

But Sara...?

Evangeline would *not* let her mistakes ruin Sara's future.

She deserved to grow up without the stigma of being born to an unwed mother. She deserved to find a man who loved her and didn't judge her for the sins her mother had committed.

Evangeline had been so naïve. She had believed everything that Jeremy had said to her. Believed that he had loved her. She wouldn't make that mistake again. Her daughter's future was too important.

She placed a kiss on Sara's head.

"She seems too young to be reading a book that advanced."

Evangeline looked up at the teasing voice. Owen approached. He wore a friendly smile. She nodded in greeting.

"Alice might've told me about your stockpile of books..." He raised his eyebrows. "With all the free time we've been granted today, I wondered if I might borrow one."

Was he flirting? She couldn't tell, and it bothered her that her judgment was so impaired from Jeremy.

Did it matter? Owen had helped her, sharing food and connecting her with Alice so she and Father and Sara wouldn't starve.

She owed him.

She settled Sara on the crate with the book in her lap and a strong warning not to move.

Owen trailed her to the back of the wagon. When Evangeline unhooked the latch on the tailgate, it threatened to topple on her. It would've, if Owen hadn't been there to catch its weight.

She worked to ignore his broad shoulder brushing her arm. Reached for the crate of books closest to her. "What kind of books do you like?"

"All kinds."

"Hmm. I've got a Dickens novel here somewhere. What about that?" She took off the guidebooks she'd been using, stacked right on top, and set them aside.

Owen still stood too close for her comfort. He reached forward and flipped the books around to see their spines.

"You read a lot, huh?"

"Mm hmm." She didn't elaborate, afraid he would take it as encouragement.

Mama was the one who'd taught her to read, not the tutors Father had hired. After Mama had passed, reading was a way to distract herself from the deep grief as well as a way to feel close to her mother.

She had been a lonely child for a long time, but her friends in the books had often kept her company.

After her debut into society, she'd been occupied with flesh-and-blood friends and parties. And then Jeremy.

During her confinement, she'd lost herself in books again to escape the grief of Jeremy's betrayal.

"Would you like to join August and me for dinner again?" Owen's question startled her out of her thoughts.

She grabbed the first book her hand touched—a dime novel—and offered it to him. "Thank you for the invitation, but Alice offered to help me tonight."

There was something in his eyes. A warmth, a small disappointment.

But he thanked her for the book and excused himself.

She was rearranging the books in their crate when motion from between their wagon and their closest neighbor—Alice's wagon—drew her attention. She leaned around the edge and found Leo, sitting with his legs bent inside his bedroll in the shade cast between the two wagons. He pushed his hat back on his head; it must've been covering his face. He looked rumpled and sleepy and she wondered whether she and Owen had woken him up.

She might've thought him lazy if she hadn't seen how very hard he worked. He'd been awake in the early morning to help her. And she knew he shared overnight watches with other men from camp. He was probably resting so he could stay awake tonight, when it counted.

He glanced up and caught her staring.

She couldn't help the flash of visceral memory of when he'd held her close on horseback.

That same connection flared to life between them now. She hadn't wanted it then, and she didn't want it now.

But she couldn't ignore him, not after he had saved Sara and her from the stream.

She still had a book in her hands, so she tipped it toward him so he could see the front cover. "Would you like to borrow something to read?"

He scowled before he averted his face, then stood up and smashed his hat on his head. "I reckon I'm too busy to have time to mess around with reading."

He strode away and left her staring after him.

Too busy to read? Was his insult against Owen or against her? She didn't know the answer, which left her feeling frustrated and embarrassed.

It was a usual occurrence around Leo, and she disliked him even more for it.

* * *

Leo stalked off away from the circled wagons toward the copse of trees a quarter mile from camp. He didn't have a destination, just needed space.

He had been this close to nodding off when he'd registered the sound of Evangeline's voice. He'd stayed in his bedroll, head on his bent arm, hat over his face, just listening to the soft tones and lyrical cadence of her voice.

Her gentleness with her sister made him think of Ma all over again. And ache...

He wanted to listen all day. He wanted to ask her to stop.

And then her father had interrupted her, asking whether they should turn around.

Yes!

No.

Ever since he'd been fifteen and his ma had passed away, leaving him in charge of Alice and the twins, he'd known what he had to do. He worked for Albert Braddock, earned his promotion to foreman, kept the family together.

He had never had such conflicting desires before.

Evangeline drove him to distraction.

He hadn't been able to stop thinking about her all day. About the weight of her in his arms, the way her eyelashes had clumped together and her eyes had flashed with vulnerability.

He'd wanted to hold her closer.

Ridiculous.

He'd spent the day riding his horse up and down the train, checking on each family as they'd crossed the shallow river. Every time he had gotten near the Murphys, his eyes inexorably tracked to her.

It didn't mean anything. When a pretty woman like Evangeline looked at him like he was her savior, it gave a man ideas. That's all.

He needed to steer clear of her.

Especially since Owen seemed to be taking an interest in her.

Leo had caught Owen's smirk in his direction after he'd quit sweet talking Evangeline about books and walked off.

Now Leo tipped his head back, looking through the canopy of green-leafed trees. He still felt hot under his skin, ashamed that he could still be embarrassed about not being able to read.

He knew his letters. But there'd been a time when Collin and Coop had been small and ma had been sick with croup for weeks. Leo had stayed home from school to help take care of the two busy toddlers.

He'd never caught up to his other classmates and been too ashamed to ask his overworked teacher for help. Once his stepfather had passed away, Leo had known his school days were over.

Their family needed more money than Ma could make as

a maid for the Braddock family. Leo didn't need to be able to read or write to work at their mill. Alice and the boys needed to stay in school.

It had been the only choice. He'd never regretted it.

And he didn't now.

But he still wanted to punch the smug grin off Owen's ugly mug. Owen had schooling. He'd had opportunities that Leo hadn't. So what?

It was their father's fault. He'd left Ma. Left Leo to fend for himself, to care for the family because he wasn't there.

And if Miss Fancy Pants wanted Owen to read her a book, Leo wasn't going to stand in the way.

He had enough to deal with riding herd on Coop. He would keep his nose out of the Murphys' business, finish his term as captain, get his family to Oregon and forget all about Miss Fancy Pants.

He strode back to camp, intending to make sure Coop was rested up for tonight's watch. Leo had purposely scheduled them together. He'd keep an eye on his brother, keep him out of trouble. He couldn't let what happened in New Jersey happen again.

He steered clear of the Murphys' wagon, which meant he entered the circle of wagons near the Fairfaxs' campsite.

Stephen was bent over his horse's hoof, though he seemed to be struggling to use the hoof pick. The horse neighed, bobbed its head and shifted, nearly stomping on the slight young man.

Stephen fell on his backside, scrambling to get out of the way as the huge black horse took two heavy steps toward him.

Leo caught the animal's lead rope before it could rear and land on Stephen. "Whoa. Easy."

The horse tossed its head before accepting Leo's hold. It *was* favoring its left foreleg.

He kept hold of the horse's halter as he held out his hand to Stephen. Stephen clamped one hand over his hat, as if to keep it attached to his head. Maybe it had gotten knocked loose when he'd fallen?

Stephen finally took Leo's hand and stood, brushing at his backside. "Thanks," he muttered gruffly as he bent to retrieve his tool.

"You need some help? Horse looks pretty uncomfortable."

"You'd think he'd be more appreciative that I'm trying to help him."

Leo rarely heard the quiet Fairfax brother speak. His voice was a little higher than Leo expected. Maybe he was more shaken up than he looked.

Leo squatted near the horse's leg, clamping its hoof between his thighs. "Some animals don't like you messing with their feet no matter how much pain they are in. Come here."

Stephen leaned in and offered the pick. Leo shook his head and pointed to where the thorn was embedded.

The horse tried to move its leg, but Leo had a good grip on him and was only rocked back, not knocked over.

Stephen reached over, seeming to avoid touching Leo in any way—even when it meant he couldn't get at the thorn adequately.

And he smelled... strange. As in, he didn't smell like body odor and trail dust, the way most of the men around camp did. Had he already gone to the creek for a bath? Seemed backwards to Leo, knowing there was still work to be done around camp.

He finally got the thorn out. Leo stood up.

Stephen backed away, head down, back to his bashful ways. "Thanks," he mumbled.

"Happy to help." Leo handed back the lead rope. The horse neighed again, but Stephen held the rope tightly and started walking.

It sounded like he was talking to the horse as he went.

Strange kid.

Collin was waving him over from their campsite, and Leo had no choice but to head that way.

His steps faltered when he caught sight of Alice and Evangeline bent over the cookpot. Alice was talking animatedly, gesturing with her hands. Evangeline looked perplexed but like she was trying to hide it.

When he joined Collin, Alice looked up at him and smiled. "Evening. Did you get your nap?"

Evangeline kept her face averted, though she had to know it was him.

"Sort of," he said.

She still didn't look at him, and Alice went back to helping her.

It was better that they kept out of each other's way.

But that mixed-up part inside of him whispered that he was wrong.

Six

"I CAN'T BELIEVE you would do this." Leo muttered as he stood over Coop with hands on his hips.

"Sorry," Coop mumbled.

"No, you aren't." Leo kicked his brother's boot a little.

Coop was drunk. Out in the woods, away from the circled wagons, Coop sat with his back against a broad tree trunk, his arms loose at his sides and his head lolled back. It was early morning, and that was a small comfort. At least no one would witness this.

Hollis had called for an early start because of the river crossing ahead. It was going to take all day to get the wagons through the dangerous, deep curve of river. But it would take two days traveling out of their way to make an easier crossing.

Leo had left camp to fetch his brother, who was supposed to be on watch while herding the cattle, running double duty.

Only Coop wasn't where he was supposed to be. Leo had tracked him down and found him like this—too drunk to be of any help. When Leo needed him the most.

Leo wanted to punch something. Namely his brother.

"You said you weren't going to do this anymore." *You promised*. Leo didn't say the words. He had wanted to trust in

Coop's promise back in New Jersey. But he hadn't. Not really. Coop had messed up too many times.

"Cou'dn't he'p m'self," Coop slurred. "I was lon'ly w' only the cows to keep me comp'ny."

Another lie. Coop didn't have to take that first drink. Leo pushed his hands through his hair, grabbing onto the too-long strands to keep from grabbing his brother and shaking him like a rag doll. He'd been doing his best to keep Coop out of sight of Braddock, and the job wrangling their cattle was meant to keep him out of trouble.

It hadn't worked.

He dropped his hands and squatted in front of Coop. "Who gave you the drink?" Leo demanded.

He and Alice and Collin had decided theirs would be a dry wagon—not a drop of alcohol on board. Not even for medicinal purposes.

He'd foolishly believed Alice's optimism about how little trouble Coop could get into on a wagon train where everyone else was a stranger. She'd wanted to believe Coop's troubles would be over if he was removed from the bad influences he'd had at home.

She'd said it would be different. That Oregon would be a new start for Coop and for their family.

But this wasn't different. This was the same old Coop making things difficult for Leo. Making things impossible.

"Who?" Leo demanded.

Coop only shook his head, wearing a smirk. All of a sudden, he went pale, leaned over, and threw up.

Thankfully, Leo had been far enough away to avoid the mess.

What was he going to do now? He'd counted on Coop for the river crossing. Someone had to man the wagon—it was the most dangerous part, so Leo had planned to do it himself. Collin and Coop would see the cattle across the river, then all three could help Alice and some of the other travelers on foot.

But Coop was too drunk to be of any use. He couldn't sit

a horse like this, much less cross the river. He'd fall off and drown.

The pressure building in Leo's chest made him want to scream. Why? Why couldn't Coop keep himself clean? Why couldn't he be a help to the family that had given up everything for him?

What was he going to do? Leo knew that when Coop got drunk like this, he would be difficult to handle. He'd fight whatever Leo asked of him. He'd even fight with his fists if he didn't like it enough.

Coop was still leaning over, though he'd stopped vomiting. And he was cackling quietly to himself.

Leo barely restrained himself again. There was nothing funny about this.

A rustling in the grass brought Leo's head up, though Coop didn't seem to register it. The last thing he needed was someone witnessing this.

Two shadows separated themselves from the surrounding trees.

"You need some help?" Owen's quiet question put Leo's hackles up.

"No. Go away."

Leo saw the twitch of Owen's shoulders in the dark, but it was August who spoke. "Alice said he can be belligerent when he's like this."

Like this, not *drunk*. The brothers somehow knew what was going on.

Bitterness rose in Leo's throat. "Alice shouldn't spread *family* business. When did she say that?"

"Right before she asked us to come out and check on you."

Asked us to come. Alice had known he was going to look for Coop. Anger rose at her meddling. She shouldn't have involved Owen or August.

"I can handle him."

And yet Leo wasn't quite so sure. The last time he'd had

to fetch a drunk Coop from a saloon, he'd gotten an elbow to the jaw and had trouble eating for a week. Coop was only an inch taller than him, but they both worked at the same strenuous job that had built muscle.

But there was another reason he didn't want his half brothers mixed up in this. He was ashamed. Ashamed that he wasn't able to handle his own family.

"No one is gonna find out about this from us," August said. He stepped forward and knelt at Coop's shoulder. "Come on now. It's time to go."

Owen moved to stand shoulder to shoulder with Leo. "We can dunk him in a little offshoot creek. It's not far. Maybe it'll sober him up a bit."

Leo gritted his teeth. The last thing he wanted to do was accept their help, but at this point, did he have a choice?

Owen went on, "I can drive your wagon, or August can push the cattle. "

They only had a single wagon between them. It frustrated Leo that he was going to have to accept their help. He still didn't want anything to do with the sons that his father had wanted, the ones he hadn't abandoned.

They pulled Coop to his feet as the first rays of sun turned the sky to gray. They were moving toward the creek when Leo noticed someone hiding behind another tree.

Evangeline, and she was close enough to have heard every word.

* * *

Evangeline shoved a bite of fried ham into her mouth as she packed Sara's bedroll into the wagon. She'd never eaten in such an uncivilized manner, but no one seemed to care on this journey.

Sara played with her rag doll next to the wagon. Evangeline had cautioned her about staying nearby during the river crossing today. Father had gone to fetch the oxen.

"Alice."

Evangeline couldn't help how she jumped or the automatic turn of her head.

It wasn't Leo, as she'd been expecting all morning, ever since she'd overheard him and his brothers in the woods. It was a man she didn't know. He wore a fine suit—or what had once been a fine suit. The black pants were ripped at one knee and the dark coat was rumpled and covered in dust, as if he'd worn it night and day and maybe been run over by a buffalo. He whipped off his hat and ran a hand through matted blond curls. Who was this?

Alice apparently hadn't heard him. She was dousing the fire she and Evangeline had cooked over this morning. The dying flames hissed and sent smoke billowing into the sky.

"Alice." He'd actually stepped into the campsite now, his hat clutched in front of him.

As the water in Alice's bucket ran out, she squared her shoulders and turned away from the spluttering ashes.

"I need to talk to you," the man said.

"I have nothing to say to you." Alice's voice was cool.

Evangeline realized she was staring and turned toward her wagon, stuffing the last of her breakfast ham into her mouth. Hadn't she learned her lesson earlier this morning?

She could still see Leo's wounded expression just before he'd realized she was there, half-hidden behind a tree. Then his expression had changed. The way he'd looked at her... a mixture of disgust and dislike.

She hadn't meant to eavesdrop then, and she didn't want to now. Alice had become a friend and lifeline over the past week.

Hoofbeats sounded, and Evangeline's heart thumped as she looked up.

Clarence Turnbull, one of the other leaders for their company, was riding on the outer edge of the campsite.

He tipped his hat, encompassing both Evangeline and

Alice with his smile. "Ten minutes before we start pulling out."

Evangeline waved to let him know she understood. She swept a giggling Sara into her arms and deposited her on the wagon seat. Father was approaching from the other direction, the oxen just behind him.

"Sit here. I'll be back in a moment to get you," Evangeline told Sara.

The man in the wrinkled suit didn't seem to be in any hurry to get back to his own wagon—wherever that was—as Alice rushed to put her cookware into an empty crate. She didn't even look his way.

He said something so quietly that Evangeline couldn't make out the words.

Alice didn't bother lowering her voice. "Go back home."

Evangeline had never heard her friend speak so coldly. Alice had an engaging sense of humor and a contagious laugh. She kept the peace between her brothers—when she could. She was genuinely kind.

The man sent a flustered glance at Evangeline, who hurriedly averted her face and moved to pick up the small pile of twigs they hadn't used in their fire this morning. No use leaving them behind when they'd want another fire tonight.

From the corner of her eye, she saw him mash his hat on his head and walk out of their camp.

Alice pretended not to notice, clanking pots as she stuffed her crate into the back of her wagon.

When she and Evangeline met near the back of the wagons, she had high color in her cheeks and her eyes were wet.

"Are you all right?" Evangeline asked.

Alice scrubbed her cheek with the back of one hand. "Yes."

She shouldn't have asked, but the words burbled out before she could stop them. "Who was that? Someone you know?"

Alice shrugged and her eyes darted away. "How well do you really know anybody? He owns the company my brothers worked for back in New Jersey. I was a maid in his grandfather's house."

She'd known that suit—stained and wrinkled as it was—was of fine quality. So the mystery man was wealthy. "Why's he on this wagon train?"

Alice shook her head, brows pulled together as her eyes flicked to Evangeline and then away again. "I don't know."

There was something she wasn't saying. Some secret hidden in the way her hands fisted at her sides.

Curiosity surged, but Evangeline wouldn't pry. Not when she needed Alice's friendship so desperately.

"Can I help you pack anything?" she asked.

Alice's smile, when it came, was wobbly. "Here's Leo now. He can help me with these last barrels."

Evangeline's cheeks went warm as Leo rode up on his horse and dismounted.

She should probably apologize for the unintended eavesdropping, but he pulled Alice aside and spoke to her in a low, urgent voice.

He didn't look Evangeline's direction once.

She should be used to it. Ever since Owen had borrowed a book from her personal library, Leo had kept his distance while in camp. Once, she'd even glimpsed him backtrack and traipse around his wagon and out of camp when he'd seen her bent close to Alice as she'd cooked over the open fire.

He didn't have to like her. They didn't have to be friends.

But she didn't want things to be awkward in camp. Without Alice, Evangeline wouldn't have any idea how to cook their meals. Alice was a font of knowledge, and she was always willing to share and to teach. And Evangeline liked Collin, and even Coop. They were kind to Sara, and even Father had warmed up to the Mason family.

She wasn't going to let any of that go simply because one man disliked her.

She would smooth things over.

Which was why she called out to him as he started leading his horse away on foot.

Alice glanced at her as she crossed toward the front of their wagon.

If Alice had heard her, surely Leo must've, too. But he kept walking.

She followed, taking several steps out into the open prairie. "Leo!"

Finally, he turned to her, the reins slack in his gloved hands. His eyes were stormy.

She hadn't been able to see him clearly this morning in the shadowed woods. Was this what he had looked like then?

"I-I didn't mean to eavesdrop. This morning."

His eyes narrowed. "Then why did you?" His words had a snap to them.

"I—" *Thought it would be more awkward if I made myself known.*

He obviously didn't want to hear her excuses. He had already turned away and gripped the saddle as if to mount up.

"I'm trying to apologize," she blurted. Which wasn't technically an apology either. "I'm sorry."

His shoulders were tense beneath the slicker he wore. The knuckles of his hand on the saddle were white.

He didn't say anything.

"I won't tell anyone. A-about Coop." Uncertainty swamped her. Had she only made things worse, reminding him of his brother's mistake? She'd wanted to reassure him, but maybe she should've stayed silent.

He stepped up into the saddle. Leather creaked as he threw his leg over the horse.

He looked down at her, hat brim throwing shadows over his eyes so she couldn't read them anymore.

"You'll want to keep a close watch on your sister today," he said in a voice so cool and unattached she felt as if she had been doused in the creek all over again. "This river is far more dangerous than a little creek."

If the chiding reminder would've been spoken between two friends, she would've been warmed by his concern.

But the way he said it... as if she was beneath his notice.

It made her feel invisible. The same way she'd felt in a crush of her former friends after Sara's birth. They'd never scorned her to her face, but it hadn't mattered because she'd known their judgment was there, just beneath the surface.

She turned away, toward her wagon, blind with tears.

It shouldn't matter.

Leo and his opinion of her shouldn't matter.

But it did.

Seven

COLLIN WAS WORRIED about Stephen Fairfax wrestling the family wagon across the river.

The young man was so slight and obviously inexperienced driving a team. He'd almost crashed his wagon into Collin's the very first day on the trail. Collin had woken from a nightmare about it the very same night, the sound of splintering wood and feeling of falling burned into his brain, even though it hadn't happened.

He knew it was a trick of his mind—if he thought about Stephen, he didn't have capacity to worry about Coop, or about Leo's fragile hold on his temper.

Collin should've stayed awake last night. It didn't matter that he'd been on watch the night before, or that the cows had been ornery all day, looking for a way to escape. He'd needed every ounce of concentration to keep them in line.

He'd been beyond exhausted, shaking with tiredness, unable to keep his eyes open.

But maybe if he'd had a cup of coffee, he could've stayed awake and talked Coop out of meeting his so-called friends. Or maybe not. Sometimes there was no talking sense into Coop.

Stephen. Think about Stephen in his wagon box on the riverbank. Thinking about Coop was too painful.

The wagons were lined up on the east side of the river, with Hollis and Clarence Turnbull guiding travelers on the best way to cross. Upstream, out of sight, Hollis had strung a long rope across the river. He'd made this crossing before and claimed it was the safest way for those traveling on foot to traverse the dangerous waters. Each person would hold on to the rope to keep them from being dragged under the fast-moving water.

Collin and Owen were downstream, pushing cattle across out of the way of the wagons. From here, they could see everything.

Every driver seemed on edge. Even the animals sensed it, as horses among the wagons whinnied, communicating their stress to each other.

"Let's get across," Owen called from a dozen yards away, the cattle between them. "Maybe we can find a little gully and stash the cattle and come back to help."

Collin nodded. He'd been in camp when Leo and his two half brothers had dragged a drunken Coop to the wagon. Coop's upper body had been sopping wet, as if they'd dunked him in the creek. He was half-asleep on his feet and reeked like a distillery.

Leo had told Collin that Owen and August had offered to help with the river crossing, and Collin had known better than to ask a bunch of questions. No doubt there'd be a family meeting later tonight, if they could find a place private enough.

Collin had expected Owen to arrive all high and mighty. But he hadn't. He'd asked Collin whether he knew how to swim—he did—and then they'd pushed the herd to the river in the quiet of dawn.

Maybe the Spencer brothers weren't so bad, though Collin would never admit as much to his older brother. But it was a kind thing they'd done this morning, helping out. They could've kept to their own wagon, could've left Leo and Collin and Alice to manage both the wagon and cattle themselves.

"Get on," Owen shouted to the cattle.

Collin pulled his hat off his head and slapped it against his thigh.

The first of the animals waded into the water, one lowing in complaint.

Collin spared a glance upriver as the cattle moved slowly. Leo's wagon was over the deep part now. The oxen were swimming in the traces, but the heavy box had become caught in the current, swept to one side.

Collin whispered a prayer.

As the nearer ox's feet touched solid ground, he gave a mighty heave. The second ox touched, too. And then they were dragging Leo and the wagon up onto dry land.

There wasn't time for jubilation because more wagons were already in the water.

Owen whistled. His horse was already shoulder-deep in the river, on the downstream side. He nudged one of the younger heifers out into the deeper water when she wanted to stay with her feet on the ground.

Collin focused on what he had to do. He splashed into the water, knowing he had to pull his own weight. For the family's sake.

Once in the water, the cattle spread apart. Owen and Collin let them have the room to swim. The water became a churning mass of hooves and unsettled thousand-pound animals, so Collin didn't mind much when Owen shouted for him to stay back.

He didn't want to be too close if one of the animals went into a panic.

Collin looked back toward the wagons, and there was the Fairfax wagon, rocking in the current. There was something about the man that made Collin uneasy. He was so slight he could've been mistaken for one of his younger sisters.

Collin had been coming back from watch yesterday morning and saw Stephen skulking around the Fairfax wagon, barely visible in the predawn light.

When the man caught sight of Collin, he ducked behind his own wagon.

The encounter, such as it was, had been strange.

Stephen was strange, as was his family. Always keeping to themselves.

The Fairfax wagon lurched. Collin watched as Stephen dropped one of the reins connected to the oxen. The young man leaned forward at a precarious angle. Collin stifled the urge to call out. It wouldn't do any good. Collin was so far down the river the other man wouldn't be able to hear him.

But if Stephen fell into the water amidst the oxen, he'd be caught underneath their hooves. Drowned, for sure.

As Stephen grabbed onto the wagon seat, his hat slipped, revealing a fall of blonde hair, down past the man's shoulders.

"Watch that one!" Owen shouted.

Collin reacted quickly, urging his horse to swim to contain a steer that was drifting too far downstream.

By the time he looked back to the Fairfax wagon, Stephen had his hat back on his head and had righted himself. He even had the reins back in his hands.

Collin blinked, telling himself to focus. He'd been so distracted by the Fairfax wagon's crossing that he'd imagined things.

Then he noticed that the wagon behind the Fairfaxs' was in trouble, too. The Murphys' wagon. He recognized Evangeline's father, with his bushy beard and fine coat.

The man had hit the same dip in the current that Stephen's wagon had. The Murphys' wagon lurched, listing to the side. The oxen panicked and pulled in opposite directions. The older man tried to right himself. Collin watched in horror as Mr. Murphy toppled off the wagon seat and into the roiling water.

* * *

Evangeline was wet and bedraggled, but she and Sara had made it across the river, thanks to the long rope and pulley that Hollis had rigged sometime before daylight.

She climbed the muddy slope on wobbly legs. Finally, she and Sara joined the group of people standing on a bluff several dozen yards upstream from the chaos of the wagons' crossing. From here, the river curved, and they had a clear view of the wagons in the turbulent water.

"How can there be crossings more difficult than this?" She didn't recognize the woman speaking.

Next to them, Irene Fairfax watched the water with a worried expression.

"The water was over my head—I nearly drowned," the unknown woman continued complaining.

Evangeline had felt a moment of panic as she'd clutched to the rope above her head. Sara had clung to her, arms wrapped tightly around her neck and legs wrapped around her waist. The ground had given way and only the strength in Evangeline's arms had kept them from being sucked into the depths of the river.

She'd flashed back to the terrifying moments in the much shallower creek a week ago.

Her fear had driven her to keep going, to keep clinging to the rope.

"Some of the crossings have ferries for hire," she murmured. Her words were as much for herself as they were for the worried stranger. "I read it in a guidebook," she said when the woman turned to her with a questioning gaze. "I'd pay almost anything not to have to do that again."

But the woman frowned. "How much? How much does it cost? We ain't made of money."

Evangeline quailed under her quick questions. "I—I don't remember. I can look it up. When my father's wagon—"

There was a gasp from someone standing at the edge of the bluff, facing the water.

"A wagon almost tipped!" Came a cry from farther away, another pocket of travelers watching.

Evangeline scooped a sopping Sara into her arms and found herself carried by the press of people who wanted to gawk at another traveler's misfortune.

The sun glared off the water, the scene almost idyllic until one glanced downriver. There, it was chaos.

One wagon spun in a slow circle, its oxen now facing the wrong direction. Two riders on horseback plunged through the water toward it. Their shouts carried on the wind, though Evangeline couldn't make out their words. Downstream from the wagons, cattle crossed. If the wagon didn't come under control, it could float down and crash through the animals making the crossing.

How awful. How frightening.

She felt again the heaviness and darkness of the water closing over her head. Fear shivered through her as she told herself she was safe. Her feet were on solid ground. The sun was bright against her skin, though she shivered.

Sara squirmed in her arms. Evangeline pressed her close. "Ssh, ssh." She rocked on the balls of her feet.

"Down!" Sara protested, grabbing a handful of Evangeline's hair from the scraggly mess that had once been a bun.

"Not yet," Evangeline said. Tensions were high, and she couldn't risk Sara getting underfoot where the wagons were exiting the river.

Evangeline squinted against the glare of sunlight off the water. Where was Father?

A wagon lurched dangerously in the center of the river, nearly toppling its driver into the water.

Right behind that wagon was Father. She recognized the

cut of his coat, even from here. His wagon lurched dangerously, too. Unlike the other driver, he didn't catch hold of the
seat.

She couldn't breathe as the seconds seemed to lengthen.
She couldn't tear her gaze away as Father dropped into the
churning waters.

No. The word caught in her throat.

She watched for Father to come back up, but he didn't.
Where was he? Did he know how to swim? Somehow she'd
never asked.

A cowboy on horseback swam forward, leaning out of his
saddle to reach for the lead oxen's harness.

Evangeline's feet were frozen to the ground. She had no
sense of anyone else around her, save Sara clutched in her
arms.

Why didn't Father appear?

More men on horses swarmed the area where Father had
disappeared. What if he got caught underneath one of the
animals?

Tears choked her, but she staved them off by sheer will. It
would help exactly no one if she broke down right now.

Holding Sara tightly to her, she began skirting the people
watching the tableau. She kept one eye on the river as she
moved.

She didn't know what she'd do once she reached the
wagons, but surely Father would be out of the water by
then—

She paused mid-step as one of the men pushing cattle
downstream gave a shout. Was that—? It looked like Collin
Mason, though she couldn't be sure from this distance. He
leaned so far off his horse that she worried he would fall in
himself. And then—somehow—he dragged her father from
the depths of the river.

Father's body was limp and unmoving. Evangeline
couldn't contain her gasp.

She'd pushed to the edge of the crowd and now broke

into a run. Sara bounced against her hip, her head banging into Evangeline's chin and making her teeth clack together so hard she saw stars.

She readjusted the girl in her arms and kept going. Was Father injured? He'd been under water for more than a minute—maybe more than two. How long could a body survive without air? She'd read so many things in preparation for this journey, but she didn't know the answer.

She was running right toward the wagons still veering out of the river. It was mayhem as drivers tried to move their frightened animals away from the water's edge. Men's voices shouted from every direction.

She didn't care.

She needed to reach Father.

And then a man on a tall, gray horse pulled up in front of her, nearly running her over.

Leo.

His face was grave. "You can't go through here on foot."

She opened her mouth to argue, then realized he had his arm extended toward her, as if he was ready to lift her onto his horse with him.

He wasn't refusing to let her through. He was trying to help her. He'd known she was so anxious to get to Father that she would've run through the moving wagons on foot.

She reached out and let him pull her up into the saddle in front of him. But this was nothing like those breathless moments at the creek.

She didn't even look at Leo. She craned her neck to see through the wagons.

"We brought your wagon out. Seems the Good Lord was smiling on you today, because none of your goods spilled into the river."

She waved off his words. "Did someone carry my father out of the water?" she demanded.

"Collin caught him as he was swept downstream."

She'd seen that much. "Is he all right?"

"I don't know." Leo's voice was grim.

Her stomach twisted as he pushed his horse into a gallop, taking them quickly between moving wagons.

She squeezed her eyes closed. What if Father was dead?

And then she forced her eyes open again. Whatever was coming, she had to face it.

Eight

LEO COULD FEEL Evangeline shaking where she rested against him on the horse.

But she didn't bow her head. She didn't cling to him. She didn't break down in sobs.

Her chin was set at a resolute angle, and though her eyes were bright with tears, none escaped to slip down her cheeks.

He drew in his horse as they approached the riverbank.

"Thank you," Evangeline said stiffly.

Thank you. After how callously he'd treated her this morning, it gave him a pang of conscience for her to say the words. His gut twisted with a sudden desire to tuck her into himself, to offer her comfort.

He didn't.

Collin was there, soaking wet. Water dripped from his elbows and his hands as he stood a few feet from Evangeline's father, who lay on the ground.

Owen was pushing the cattle farther from the riverbank but shot a look over his shoulder.

Hollis and Maddie Fairfax knelt beside Mr. Murphy on the muddy ground. How had she gotten over here?

James Murphy wasn't moving.

Leo feared the worst.

He'd been swimming, clinging to his horse's saddle when he'd seen the man fall in the river. Helpless to reach him, as he'd been upriver and the current swift, Leo had been quick to reach the oxen team and guide them to the riverbank, but that had been more to keep the animals from bumping into another wagon or creating havoc in the middle of the river.

He wished he could've done more.

"Let me down, please," Evangeline whispered.

Leo reined in and handed her down from the horse, quickly following. He threw his reins over a branch of a small scrub oak nearby.

"Let me have your sister." Maybe he should've made it sound more like a suggestion than an order, because her eyes flashed when she turned back to him.

"She doesn't need to watch," he murmured quietly.

She nodded with a trembling lip, handing Sara into his arms. He felt the tremor in her hand when it brushed his biceps.

He hung back as Evangeline lifted her skirts and ran to where her father lay.

Sara lifted her head, looking straight into Leo's face. He didn't want her looking for Evangeline, so he pointed to the water's edge.

"Look there. See that big bird?" It was a heron, maybe, or a crane. He didn't know. He only knew it stood in the water with long legs and beak. "Maybe later your sissy can tell you all about it with her book."

He wished that for Sara. Prayed that her father would be all right so that Evangeline could read her silly books.

Sara gripped the shoulder of his shirt with her little fist. She stared at the bird without speaking.

A loud cough erupted before the distinct sound of vomiting.

Leo glanced over his shoulder to see James lying on his side spewing all the river water he must've taken in.

He was alive.

Evangeline knelt beside him, uncaring of the mud and filth. Silent tears streamed down her cheeks. The man's face was pale as death, though two red spots bloomed in his cheeks as his body fought to expel the water.

Several voices shouted from behind Leo, the cacophony they'd left behind only moments ago becoming louder.

Hollis stood up, his focus already on the next disaster. "Mason, you help get him back to his wagon."

Maddie Fairfax kept supporting James, leaning over him to ask a quiet question that Leo didn't hear.

Evangeline looked up, her worried gaze swinging from the wagon master to Leo. He held her stare as he crossed the space to join her, Sara in his arms.

He went to one knee, down by James's ankles, gently setting Sara on her feet. She immediately threw herself into Evangeline's arms.

Evangeline rested her chin on the girl's head. They were close, the two sisters. In the past days, he'd seen how Evangeline doted on her much-younger sister, how she watched out for her and took care of her. It couldn't be easy, traveling on a difficult journey like this without the girls' mother, but Evangeline was doing all right.

But how would she manage over the next few days with an injured father?

"He okay?" Leo murmured.

He was now lying on his back. Maddie prodded at his midsection, and he groaned.

"I think he's broken a rib or two," Maddie said.

"What're you doing over here?" he asked.

Evangeline shot him a look that said she wanted to wallop him. He'd seen that look many a time from Alice.

Maddie didn't look up from James. "Back in Ireland, my mum was a healer. I've helped her."

That was better than nothing. James needed a doctor, though they didn't have one traveling with their wagon train.

"That hurts," James snapped when she touched his side again. He looked haggard, his skin gray.

"He was probably thrown into something while he was under water." Maddie murmured to Evangeline. "Maybe a submerged branch or a boulder."

"We need to get him up," Leo said, earning another one of those looks from Evangeline.

James was obviously shaken and hurt, but Hollis had told them to get him back into his wagon. More cattle were making the crossing now. Leo didn't want anybody getting trampled.

"Can you support his other side?" Leo asked Maddie. He nodded to Evangeline. "Keep a tight hold on that one."

Her eyes flashed again. He hadn't meant it as a poke at her, not like he had earlier.

Evangeline swept Sara into her arms as Leo linked his hands under James's armpit and pulled the man to his feet.

Halfway there, James bent over as a coughing fit overtook him. More water spewed from his lips. He clutched his left side, pale and spent.

Leo had to hold him upright. Maddie steadied him from the opposite side.

"All right?" Leo asked.

James only groaned.

"Lean on me," Leo said when the older man nearly lost his footing. "We'll get you back to your wagon and you can lie down."

If there was room inside on top of all Evangeline's books.

"'Vangeline drive de wagon?" Sara's sweet voice rang out over the sounds of James's struggling breaths.

Leo glanced over and saw the trepidation on Evangeline's face. She didn't know how to drive a team. And no book was going to tell her how taxing it would be—if she even had the strength.

"I'll be fine—" But James couldn't even finish his sentence. He clamped his mouth closed as a step jarred him.

"You need to rest," Maddie said. "And let those ribs heal." She shook her head slightly at Leo. The man couldn't walk, much less be able to drive a team.

"We'll find someone to help you get the wagon moved for tonight." By now, Coop had had a couple of hours to sleep off his drink. Leo wanted to dunk him in the river, but he'd ply him with a cup of coffee instead and force him to drive Evangeline's wagon. It was the least Coop could do after letting everyone down this morning.

"You sad?" Sara asked.

This time when Leo glanced, her little palm was resting on Evangeline's cheek.

Evangeline looked worried but steadied her expression and managed to smile at the girl. "I'm not sad. We'll be all right."

She was lying. Even he could see that.

He could admit to himself that she was more resilient than he'd given her credit for on those first days out of Independence. He'd never heard her utter one whisper of complaint about the long days walking. She'd traded a fine shawl to Alice for the initial cooking lessons—and then they'd become fast friends.

She did whatever Alice asked, or Hollis. Whatever was needed.

But would she be able to keep up with her father incapacitated?

* * *

That night, Evangeline eased out of the wagon, trying to jostle the conveyance the least amount possible as she took the last step from the tailgate to the ground.

The camp was quiet around her. Darkness had fallen. Only a few campfires remained, burning low.

It seemed everyone was frightened and exhausted after the river crossing. One wagon had toppled completely and washed down the river. The driver had survived, but that family had no supplies. Nothing left. They were dependent on charity. Tomorrow, when she could think straight, she would measure out some beans and coffee to give to them.

Evangeline took two steps to the tent where Sara slept. She peeked inside the flap, careful not to make much movement. She could see the dark outline of Sara sleeping with her rump in the air, and hear her soft, steady breaths.

Sara was all right.

Evangeline pressed one hand to her mouth as she gently closed the tent flap. She turned away, rushing several steps into the darkness outside the ring of wagons.

Long prairie grasses tickled her ankles as she bent over. Pressing her skirts against her face to mask the sound, she finally let go of the tenuous hold on her emotions and great, heaving cries escaped her.

Sara was all right.

But Father wasn't.

His ribs were bad. Worse than he wanted to admit. His body kept surprising him with coughs at unexpected moments, and when a cough seized his body, he went stiff with pain.

And he was running a low fever. She'd left him with a cool washrag on his forehead, like he was a little child and she was the parent.

What was she going to do?

Father couldn't drive the wagon. Maybe she could learn, but then who would watch over Sara? The wagon was filled with the supplies they'd carefully packed, full to the brim. With father in the wagon, there wasn't room for Sara, too. She was a child, too young to understand she couldn't jostle Father.

They couldn't go home. Not only could Evangeline not face that river crossing again, but she couldn't see a way to drive them back to civilization.

This was all her fault. She'd stubbornly insisted that the

journey would be uneventful. And now Father was badly injured.

She attempted to stifle the tears, stop her crying. She dried her face with her skirts, but more tears came.

The night sky mocked her with its perfection, a million stars glittering like diamonds against a velvet background.

She felt so small. And so afraid.

What was she going to do?

Footsteps in the grass alerted her to someone approaching.

"It's me." Came a male voice in the dark.

Leo.

The last man she wanted to see right now. He'd been surprisingly kind earlier, but she would never forget his disdain.

But she was too tired, too frightened to muster anything more than the energy she needed to stop her tears.

"Sara all right?"

She cleared her throat. "She's sleeping. I think Alice wore her out today." Leo's sister had been quick to offer to watch over Sara while Evangeline had tended to Father. She'd checked on them once during the afternoon and found the pair giggling over a tiny handful of dough. Alice had had the brilliant idea to give Sara a pinch off the loaf she was making for supper.

Alice was good with Sara. She was good with everyone, drawing in strangers as if they were friends.

But Evangeline couldn't depend on Alice's charity. Caring for Sara every day was a job in itself. Alice had enough to do.

"And your father?" Leo asked, a darker shadow against the night sky.

She shook her head, tears choking her all over again. She didn't want to cry in front of him. Didn't want him to see her weakness, how scared she was.

"Did Coop say anything to you? I told him to keep his trap shut."

She took a half-gasping breath. She could talk about Coop. "He was fine. Kind, even." He'd mostly kept to himself, though he'd checked on her a couple of times as she'd tended Father in the stuffy covered wagon.

"And you?" His quiet words didn't make any sense until he elaborated. "How are you?"

A soft sob burst from her lips, unexpected and unwanted.

Before she could make some excuse or run away, he'd crossed the last couple of feet between them. His broad hand closed around her elbow and he pulled her close.

She imagined pushing him away, but only for a second. His shoulder was broad beneath her cheek, and she found herself crying into his shirt.

He held her loosely, and she leaned into him, emotion crashing over her as if a river of sadness and fear was pulling her under.

She drew in a breath, thinking she could stave off more tears, only to gulp and wheeze.

His hand came up to press against the base of her skull as he pulled her closer.

She would never be able to look the man in the face again, not after this.

He held her until her sobs quieted, until she was breathing more steadily. She would never have imagined him capable of such tenderness.

Finally, she stepped away, brushing the last of the tears from her face with her fingers.

"Better now?" he asked.

"I don't know." She felt... empty. "I'm certainly humiliated." She hadn't meant to admit to that.

A short pause grew between them. "Then maybe it makes us even."

What?

Oh. He meant this morning, when she'd witnessed him and Coop. That felt like a lifetime ago.

"I'm sorry I said what I did about your sister." His quiet words sounded sincere in the darkness. "Little kids get curious. Collin used to wander off all the time when he was Sara's age. What happened at the creek wasn't your fault. You're a wonderful big sister to her."

She was so stunned that it took longer than it should've to loosen her tongue from the top of her mouth. "Thank you."

Was that what he'd come out here for? To make an apology?

She was so tired and heartsick that she couldn't think straight, couldn't figure out his motives.

He drew in a breath, as if he wanted to say something more.

But he didn't, and the silence between them grew to something almost palpable. What did one say after crying all over a man who was mostly a stranger?

"You should get some rest," he said finally. "Tomorrow will be a long day."

"What about you?"

"I'm headed to my bedroll, too. I've got the last watch of the night, so I'll catch a few hours of sleep now."

"Would you teach me how to drive the wagon?" she blurted.

He was silent for a beat too long. "I'll help you figure something out."

It wasn't agreement.

But she was too tired to argue. She went to her tent and lay down beside Sara.

As she drifted off to sleep, she felt phantom arms around her, broad shoulders big enough to help carry her burdens.

Nine

EVANGELINE FELT as if she had barely closed her eyes when she woke. It was dark—the kind of full darkness that one *felt* inside. It must still be the middle of the night.

But the perfect solution had jolted into Evangeline's mind. That's what had woken her.

She slipped out of the tent and knelt for a moment to affix the tiny string and bell she'd rigged to the tent flap in case a situation like this happened again. If Sara woke and opened the tent flap, the bell would ring, and Evangeline would hear.

She straightened and tiptoed to the family wagon.

Every campfire in their circle of wagons had died to coal or ashes. She hesitated only briefly.

She needed to act now. What she was going to do couldn't wait—and she couldn't risk having witnesses.

She unlatched the wagon's tailgate as slowly as she could, her breath catching when the metal latch scraped softly.

From inside the wagon, Father coughed. Once, twice, and she stood frozen. But he didn't stir other than that. She strained her ears. Was his breathing more labored than usual? Her resolve solidified. This was the right thing to do.

Father was injured. Maybe sick. She couldn't drive a wagon one mile by herself. Much less the thousand that they still needed to reach Oregon.

She needed help.

And there was one surefire way to get it.

Money.

She lowered the tailgate inch by painstaking inch, until it hung on its own. She raised on her toes and reached... there. Father had put a false floorboard in the wagon. The tips of her fingers slid into the crack where the wagon bed should be smooth. It was usually covered with her heavy crates of books, but last night she'd been in a hurry, and Father sleeping in the wagon bed had meant all their supplies had to be shifted.

Her unconscious had remembered the crack, had shown her this solution as she'd slept.

She pried the small board free. Leaning her elbows on the edge of the wagon, she held the board with one hand and reached the other inside. Her fingers met the smooth stacks of gold coins Father had carefully packed. Two thousand dollars worth.

Underneath the coins were the bank notes that Father had cashed out. All of the research she'd done had revealed there were no banks in the Oregon Territory. Not yet. Father had risked everything by cashing out his equity in his Boston businesses.

And it was all hidden in this secret compartment in the wagon. He'd warned her not to breathe a word of it. She wouldn't.

But she was going to use some of it.

She filled one fist with coins, careful not to let them clink together. It was more difficult to wedge the floorboard back into place with only one hand, but she managed it.

She slowly moved the nearest crate—too light to be books —on top of the space, where the crack couldn't be noticed.

As she slowly raised the tailgate, Father moaned. Compassion stirred. Worry, too. Would he recover?

She would ask Maddie to check on Father in the morning. Maybe a poultice would help clear whatever remained in his lungs. Mrs. Fletcher had made them in the past, but she wasn't here now. And though Maddie had been reticent to share much, the way she'd wrapped Father's chest spoke of much practice.

With the tailgate securely latched, she turned outward. Leo had mentioned he would have the last watch.

She didn't think it was close to dawn. The air held a chill only felt in the middle of the night.

Which meant Leo might still be sleeping.

His family shared a tent. She didn't see how they had any room inside, with four of them. Alice had insisted on parking their wagon next to Father's wagon, which mean the Masons' tent was close.

But if Evangeline called out for Leo, someone else might wake up. She didn't want to be overheard.

She could wait inside her own tent until she heard him stirring, but what if she fell back to sleep?

She wanted this resolved now.

She vacillated on what to do, standing in the shadow of her own wagon, near invisible.

And then a hulking figure separated from the darkness. Footsteps crunched lightly in the prairie grass as the figure approached the camp.

Her heart beat frantically in her chest. It was ignorant to be out alone like this. Did she have a choice? Not much of one.

She gathered her courage and stepped away from the wagon.

The figure went still. She could almost sense the watchfulness of whoever it was.

"Leo?" she whispered.

"No. It's Coop."

Coop. Her pulse pounded. She wasn't afraid of him, but she'd counted on finding Leo, not his brother.

89

"Everything okay?" he whispered. He didn't sound drunk, not like the way he'd slurred his words when she'd overheard him two nights ago. Was he coming back from time spent on watch? Or had he been away from camp for some other—less noble—purpose?

"Yes," she whispered back. "I mean, no. I need to speak to Leo."

Coop kept his distance, still nearer the Masons' tent than her. "I'll wake him for you."

Coop bent and slipped inside. There was a soft murmur of voices, the sound of fabric rustling, another whisper.

And then Leo's figure separated from the tent, tall and broad in the darkness.

Her heart seemed to be pounding for another reason as he strode toward her in the darkness.

He reached for her, his hands going to her upper arms. She was surprised. That was the only reason she let him pull her close.

One fist and one open hand pressed against his rumpled, untucked shirt. Would his hair look just as rumpled as his shirt felt? He smelled of man. She caught his quick yawn and the crack of his jaw.

"What's the matter?" he asked, his voice a low rumble.

Would he have pulled her close like this if it'd been daylight? Surely he must still be half asleep.

"I need to talk to you," she whispered.

"Something wrong with your father? Sara?"

She shook her head twice, her forehead brushing his chin. He'd rushed out of bed to help her. Her idea solidified in her mind. This was going to work.

She would step away, but she didn't want to be overheard.

"What is it then?" He sounded perplexed, not angry. Still warm and sleepy.

Her mind played a cruel trick on her, reminding her of another time and place, another pair of arms embracing her. Jeremy had once promised to always take care of her.

She suddenly felt as if she'd been doused in cold water. Those were *not* the type of thoughts she needed to be thinking right now. This was a business transaction, nothing more.

"Not here," she said. "I don't want to be overheard."

Coop was still awake inside their tent, wasn't he? But she also wanted an excuse to take a step back from Leo.

He grunted but took her arm and led her out into the darkness, away from the camp.

As soon as she judged they were out of hearing distance, she blurted, "I want to pay you to take my family to Oregon."

She winced, thankful he couldn't see her face in the darkness. That had lacked finesse.

"I don't understand," he said gruffly.

"It makes perfect sense," she rushed. "You need money." She'd overheard that much when he'd berated Coop. "I have money."

She reached out in the darkness, took one of his big hands in hers. Maybe his sleepiness made him malleable, because he let her turn his palm toward the sky, let her fill his hand with the gold coins she'd taken from her wagon. She pressed his fingers until they closed over the money, ignoring the warmth of his skin against hers.

She swallowed hard. "It's perfect."

* * *

Leo stood dumbfounded, staring into the darkness.

He'd been rousted from a deep sleep to Coop's whispered, "Evangeline needs you," and he still wasn't fully awake, his brain sluggish and slow.

He still felt the shape of her burned into his memory. Had it been instinct or something he didn't want to admit even to himself that had prompted him to reach for her in his half-awake state?

"Start at the beginning," he said.

He heard her inhale. "You said yourself that Father won't be able to drive the wagon. I can learn how to do it, but there is so much else. Taking care of Sara and now Father. Feeding the oxen. Driving the team. Cooking supper. I can't do everything on my own."

"Why not ask Owen? He seems sweet on you. He wouldn't even need to be paid. Or someone else." His gut twisted when he said it.

He felt some motion in the darkness, as if she had waved her hand. He could perfectly imagine the dismissive gesture. "That's why you're the perfect man for the job. The two of us would never suit. There are too many things you don't like about me. And—"

He waited for her to list off all the reasons he wasn't suitable for her, but she remained silent. He stood in the darkness, his face burning.

"I don't know whether or not to be offended," he admitted.

"I didn't mean to offend you," she said quickly. "I only meant—"

He waited. And then waited some more for her to say something. Maybe apologize.

But what she said was, "I'll pay you two thousand dollars to get my family to Oregon."

That made him clamp his mouth shut. The weight of coins in his hand felt heavier.

"There are more gold coins in a compartment in our wagon. I can pay you five hundred dollars now and the rest when we reach the Willamette valley. I didn't count that, it was dark."

"Two thousand dollars?" he croaked. He'd known she and James were well-off. It couldn't be more obvious from their fine clothes and brand-new wagon. But a secret compartment? Gold coins?

"Who else knows about the money?" Gossip tended to

spread through the wagon train like wildfire. Two days ago, a little boy had been bitten by a snake while walking alongside his mother. Leo had heard about it sitting around the fire eating supper.

"No one. When Father liquidated—"

"Don't tell me," he interrupted her. "I don't want to know."

How had Evangeline and James kept a secret this big?

Two thousand dollars. That much money would allow him to get Alice and Coop and Collin settled. He could buy them a castle with that kind of money. He'd planned to help them build a house, put in a garden, raise cattle. He'd known it was going to take years.

But with this kind of money, Collin and Coop could start a business. Alice could have a nice house, built to her specifications.

There had to be a catch.

"A lot of things can happen on the trail. More river crossings. Buffalo stampede. Sickness. What if —" What if James didn't survive the injuries he'd sustained today? Leo couldn't say the words.

She did. "What if we don't make it to Oregon?" Her voice was quiet, pensive. "If you put in all the effort, I won't hold it against you if there is a natural disaster or we get cholera. You'll still be paid."

"Why me?" There had to be a half dozen men that would be willing to help Evangeline. She'd witnessed him with his drunken lout of a brother.

Knew he was desperate.

It made a bitter taste in his mouth.

"The men trust you," she said. "I've seen the way you've handled conflicts between travelers. I trust you."

I trust you.

The two of us would never suit.

Something wasn't making sense here, but his brain was

too muddled with the thought of all that money—enough to buy his freedom—and the sleep he was missing.

She'd pricked his pride saying they didn't suit.

So what?

Was he going to let pride get in the way of two thousand dollars? *No.*

His sluggish brain finally fed him an idea.

"If we do this, we don't want anyone getting wind that it's a business arrangement. It's dangerous for you and for your sister if anybody knows you've got that kind of money."

"Agreed," she said quickly. "So you'll do it?"

"I'm not sure you're going to like my condition."

"What condition?"

"If we're keeping our arrangement a secret, we'll need to give everyone a reason to think I would be near you all the time. More than simply helping out."

"You're our captain. Isn't that reason enough?" She sounded stiff and uncomfortable. And maybe it was wrong of him to feel a bit of glee.

"It'd be more believable if we play-act that I am your beau."

She was silent.

"You know it's not real. So do I. But to everyone else, we are courting. No one will question it."

She still didn't say anything, and he wondered for a moment whether his pride and his suggestion had lost him the chance for that cash.

But then her voice came stiff and cold in the darkness. "Fine."

She'd agreed. Maybe he would regret it when he was fully awake or tomorrow morning, when she couldn't hide that little displeased frown. But for now, he could almost taste the freedom of knowing that his siblings were settled and well taken care of.

"You should get some rest," he said. "I've got to go on watch."

He sensed more than saw her nod in the darkness. "I'll walk you back to your tent."

She hesitated. Was she rethinking the whole thing?

"Good night," she muttered.

And it was. A night offering him a whole new start.

Ten

"DO you need some help with the wagon today?" Owen asked.

Evangeline looked up from the knot of leather straps tangled in her hands. She knelt in the trampled grass, an open book at her side, attempting to unwind the lines that somehow attached to the oxen's harness.

She hadn't seen or heard from Leo yet this morning. Had he changed his mind in the bright light of day?

Owen stopped a few feet away, charming smile in place, hat in his hand. He appeared ready to help with whatever she needed.

She let her gaze fall to the open book and the sketch on the page that showed a pair of oxen hitched to a wagon. "I thought it would be easier to figure this out."

It wasn't an answer. It was a distraction.

Sara sat by her side, munching on a biscuit from Alice. When Evangeline looked to the little girl, needing an excuse to avoid Owen's too-perceptive eyes, Sara mumbled something unintelligible with her mouth full and waved the biscuit.

"You'll need a driver for your wagon," Owen said. She should've known he wouldn't be deterred.

A shadow fell over her as strident footsteps drew near. "I'm driving Evie's wagon today."

Leo had his arms crossed, his expression inscrutable as he stared at his brother. And then he glanced down at her, and his eyes softened somehow. He didn't smile, not really, though the corners of his mouth pulled.

Leo reached out his hand. Evangeline was more than happy to abandon the mess of leather to take it.

He pulled her to her feet. His hand fell away and there they stood. Next to each other but not touching.

"*Evie?*" Owen repeated.

Evangeline forced herself to look away from Leo and smile at Owen, forced herself not to show any distaste. She disliked nicknames, and that one in particular. She'd told off a tutor as a young child for not using her full name. The woman had nearly been fired.

Owen's narrowed-eye gaze darted back and forth between her and Leo.

This was never going to work. She wasn't good at pretending.

But before she could expose the whole farce, Sara threw herself at Leo, wrapping her arms around his right leg, biscuit forgotten on the ground.

Leo swung her up into his arms, a dazzling smile changing his face completely. "Hullo, you." He tapped her nose with his index finger.

"Leo dwive da wagon."

"That's right, punkin. Maybe you can sit up there and help me for a bit."

Sara squealed and clapped her hands.

Owen cleared his throat. Evangeline jerked. She'd been so caught up watching Leo with Sara that she'd nearly forgotten his half brother.

She attempted to school her features, unsure of what had leaked out in her expression.

Owen looked thoughtful. His gaze swung to Leo. "You and the twins need any help with the cattle today?"

Somehow, Leo had shifted to stand closer to her. They still weren't touching, but she was aware of the heat of his body and the sheer breadth of him at her shoulder.

"Collin has the cattle today. He won't need any help."

It was a clear dismissal, and Owen must've known it. Nothing showed on his face as he tipped his hat at Evangeline. "Maybe I'll check on you tonight. See if you need any help then."

At her elbow, Leo seemed to grow even larger. Before he could say anything, she reached out and touched his arm.

"That's very kind," she said.

Owen turned and strode away. She was left with Leo, who stared down at where her hand still rested on his forearm.

She jerked away.

He tipped his head toward the wagon. "I'll get the oxen hitched."

She turned to scoop up her book. His sharp eyes missed nothing, and his mouth had turned down in a frown. He must think her a ninny for not knowing how to do simple tasks. For needing a book to explain things.

"I don't think this is going to work," she whispered as she scurried to stay beside him.

"Maybe you shouldn't frown at me," he muttered.

"You called me Evie." She barely resisted the urge to *thwap* him with her book. "I hate that nickname."

His eyes glittered down at her, like he was pleased she'd given him something to bug her about. But he didn't say anything more as he deposited Sara on the ground behind the wagon, where they were more hidden from prying eyes.

"I'm driving your wagon."

Why had he said that? It's what they'd agreed to.

He looked at her expectantly. She didn't know what to say.

"That's what you tell anyone who asks."

Ah. He'd overheard Owen's question.

What had happened in the night almost seemed a dream in the light of day. She hadn't fully trusted him to see it through.

He seemed to see that thought cross her mind and something shuttered in his expression.

For the first time, she noticed the exhausted lines fanning his eyes and mouth. A pink line extended from the neckline of his shirt and up his neck, almost to his jaw, as if he'd been sleeping hard. She knew he'd had an early-morning watch. But apparently the first thing he'd done after waking was come to check on her.

Something twisted uncomfortably inside her.

"I'd like to learn to drive the wagon," she murmured, changing the subject.

He turned away and began to unpack the crates and supplies she'd stashed in the wagon bed this morning. The tent was a wad of fabric bundled on top. She hadn't been able to fold it properly without Father's help and with Sara jumping on top of the canvas at every opportunity.

She burned a little with embarrassment for him to see her incompetence.

"How's your father this morning?" He asked the question without looking at her, and she couldn't help but notice that he hadn't answered her, either.

He didn't take the tent out, just tucked it in as he re-packed the items he'd moved.

"His fever is worse, I think. He had a coughing fit so violent that I thought he might break another rib. I meant to go and ask Maddie if she knew of a poultice I could make, but I didn't have time."

And apparently the time she'd spent packing the wagon hadn't been good enough, judging by the way he was moving every box she'd touched.

"Why don't you go to her now? Camp'll be breaking soon, but there's still time while I get the oxen in their traces."

She got a little caught in the warmth in his eyes. No doubt he was only concerned for Father because of the reward he would receive at the end of the trail.

She reached for Sara's hand, but he stopped her. "I can watch over her."

She wrinkled her brows. "Won't she be in the way?"

The gentle way he looked at Sara made something warm unfurl inside her. "We'll make do. I got used to doing chores with a little one following me around."

What did that mean?

She didn't have time to ask because the bugle blared once. A warning that they'd be pulling out soon.

Evangeline couldn't help looking over her shoulder as she hurried to the Fairfax's wagon. Leo lifted Sara onto his shoulders and was whistling as he strode away to fetch the oxen.

She couldn't make him out. One minute he was as prickly as a cactus, the next he was tenderhearted with a rambunctious little girl.

And she was a little afraid she was beginning to like both sides of him.

* * *

"This doesn't seem so hard."

At Evangeline's words, Leo glanced up from where he'd settled Sara on his knee.

The wagon box was narrow and that meant he and Evangeline were shoulder-to-shoulder and hip-to-hip on the narrow bench seat.

She had the reins looped around her shoulders and feet braced against the floorboard. She looked so serious that he wanted to reach over and ruffle her hair or tweak her ear or something.

"It'll wear on you after a day in the seat," he told her.

She shot him a glance from the side of her eye but otherwise kept her gaze forward.

Afternoon sunlight slanted across her face and lit up the faint pink sunburn high on her cheeks. He couldn't help noticing her pretty face. Her fancy dress hadn't held up to the rigors of the trail. There was a mended spot at the hem and one near her knee.

He'd been in the unfortunate position of having to watch her nearly all day. He hadn't realized the monotony of driving one of these wagons. Up until now, he'd been on horseback most of the day, checking on whoever needed help.

But thanks to Evangeline's plan, he'd left his horse tied up behind his family wagon and been in this seat all day.

He'd watched her gather armloads of wood, keeping Sara interested by giving the child her own small load to carry. Twigs were scarce with all the other wagon trains collecting, too, but Evangeline must've scoured every inch of ground because she'd pulled in a decent load.

Those first days on the trail, Leo had convinced himself that she was some kind of society darling. A spoiled, High and Mighty princess. He'd thought she wouldn't make it a week.

But everything he'd seen over the past few days had refuted his earlier opinion.

In the midst of her daily tasks, she took time to teach her sister all manner of things. While they were eating a cold meal of jerky and breakfast leftovers, she'd count with her fingers. While they walked and collected firewood, she pointed out tiny details. She was like a book herself, full of facts about everything from snails to frogs to the constellations in the night sky.

She was so smart that he felt witless being around her.

Why had he thought teaching her to drive the wagon would be a good idea? Being close to her made him feel like a dunce.

He'd felt sorry for her, that was it. She'd been carrying a drooping Sara on her shoulder, and he'd watched as every blink of the little girl's eyes had grown longer and longer.

Evangeline wouldn't have asked for help; she would've carried the dead weight of a sleeping toddler for as long as she'd needed.

He'd been sitting up here in the wagon seat twiddling his thumbs. One quick stop had been all he'd needed to get Evangeline into the seat next to him. He now had Sara's warm, solid weight resting against his chest. She was almost asleep.

With one arm around the tot, he could still reach out and help Evangeline with the reins if she needed it.

Evangeline glanced at him uncertainly. "Are you certain you don't want her to lie down in the back?"

"She's fine here. And we don't have to worry about her jostling your father."

Plus, having Sara on his lap gave him something to focus on other than Evangeline beside him.

He was a little worried that James's cough seemed to be getting worse throughout the day. And that he continued to run a fever. On Maddie's advice, he and Evangeline had stopped the wagon mid-morning to have the older man sit up for a while. That had helped his cough, but his ribs had pained him so much that he'd laid down again soon after.

Evangeline cared for him patiently, providing him food and water and bathing his forehead with a cool, damp rag. James had been in such pain that he had barely spoken.

"Am I doing it correctly?" She asked from her seat beside him. "It feels as if I'm doing something wrong."

"It's pretty hard to get it wrong." But he looked her over, quickly skimming his gaze away from the pretty curve of her cheek. "You'll want to relax your posture some or your back will be all twisted up tonight."

She shrugged her shoulders once but still sat stiff and upright, like she was tied to a post or something. "Like this?"

"It's not a ballroom dance. You can slouch a little in the seat." Not that he'd ever been to one of the fancy dances Rob Braddock and his grandpa gave occasionally. He'd once been leaving the powder mill at the same time Braddock had been exiting his house dressed in a suit like a peacock. Leo had been covered in charcoal dust and exhausted from the day's work. At the time, Leo couldn't imagine anything worse than dressing up in starched, uncomfortable clothes and being forced to rub elbows with folks he didn't even like.

Did Evangeline like fancy balls and dressing up?

He didn't have time to wonder about it before he noticed a group of women walking several dozen yards to the north. One figure separated from the others, clearly heading their way. Alice.

His sister had been entirely too curious when he had informed her he was going to be driving Evangeline's wagon today. He wished he could predict what she was going to say now as she approached to walk next to his side of the wagon.

"Driving lessons?" Alice asked.

"Yes." The bright tone in Evangeline's voice was in direct contrast to the sudden tension in her body—tension he could feel because of how close they sat. "Your brother is as patient as you are over the cookpot."

Alice's gaze skipped from Evangeline to Leo, her lips pursed slightly in a thoughtful way. Sara had gone limp against him.

"I knew there was something between the two of you," she murmured. "The grumpy expression you wear every time you've been around her was too obvious."

His face grew hot, and he could only hope Evangeline couldn't hear over the scrape of the wagon wheels against the hard ground.

But he needed Alice to believe that what was between him and Evangeline was genuine, so he smiled at his sister.

She leaned past him to throw her next words at Evangeline. "He's always been good with little children."

"Oh. Um..." Evangeline glanced at him, at Sara who let out a tiny snore against his arm. Something in her expression softened. He knew it was for Sara, for the little sister Evangeline adored.

But it still twisted him up inside.

"When Coop and Collin were that age, Leo spent hours playing horsey with them."

Alice's words broke the tenuous connection, and he realized he'd been staring at Evangeline like a lovestruck pup. What was he doing?

He squinted, focusing on a point just past the lead ox's head. "It'd be nice if they still looked up to me now like they did back then."

Alice made some kind of disparaging noise. "They do."

He didn't want to talk about Coop right now. The frustration of finding his brother drunk and unruly was still too raw. And Evangeline must've known it, too.

"I always wanted a sister," she said wistfully.

"Me too." Alice sent Leo a mischievous wink. "Maybe someday I'll get one."

Part of him itched with the desire to set her straight, but he clenched his back teeth against the urge.

"I'll see you in camp for supper," his scamp of a sister said. Then she slowed her steps and bent to pick up a twisted piece of kindling.

He felt hot under the collar.

Beside him, Evangeline was quiet. Was she thinking about Coop? What kind of woman would want to attach herself to a man with a mess for a family?

They were only playing pretend. If this thing between them had been real, he couldn't see how it would work.

Evangeline leaned out and glanced behind the wagon. Turned back to face forward. "Why didn't you tell her?" she asked quietly.

"Tell her what?"

"That this," she gestured between the two of them with one hand before quickly returning it to the reins, "isn't real. You seem close. I thought you might've told her."

He noticed the wagon a dozen yards in front of them veering to the left. There might be something in the path they needed to avoid. When Evangeline didn't change the oxen's trajectory, he reached over and touched her wrist, guiding the movement of her hand until the oxen responded.

"We are close," he said. "And she's close to our brothers."

When her expression looked puzzled, he went on, "It puts you at risk if more people know about your fortune. There are some unscrupulous folks on this journey. Someone might take advantage or try to steal from you. The fewer people who know about that gold, the better."

He didn't like to think it, but he didn't want to risk Coop being mixed up in something like that. His brother wouldn't steal, but he had a habit of falling in with the wrong friends. If he knew Evangeline had gold hidden in her wagon, he might get drunk and let it slip to one of his so-called friends. At this point, Leo didn't even know who they were.

"Why don't you like Owen? Or August?"

The mention of Owen immediately brought a scowl to his face. There was a reason he'd suggested she wrangle Owen into her plan. She liked him, gravitated toward him even.

"You're so protective of Alice and the twins, I wondered... but you don't have to tell me."

The last thing he wanted to do was talk about this.

But it also irked him that she'd given him an out. *You don't have to tell me.*

"The man who fathered me left us when Alice was an infant. He went west for a grand adventure. A year later, he sent her divorce papers. She remarried the twins' father. We never saw my father again."

He said the words in a matter-of-fact manner, trying to keep bitterness from his voice.

"He chose California, and he chose to father Owen and August. I didn't even know they existed until a few months ago."

She was quiet. Did she regret asking now that she knew about the whole sordid affair?

"Is he still alive?"

"No." His answer had sharp edges. She shifted slightly on the seat.

"Is that why you aren't married?" she blurted, looking surprised at herself. "Because you're too busy taking care of your siblings?"

"You think it's because I have no prospects?"

Her eyes flitted to him and then away. Pink roses bloomed in her cheeks. "Why would I think that?"

He was hit with a bolt of the same attraction he'd felt when he'd pulled her from that creek days ago.

It felt dangerous. So he asked, "Why aren't you married?"

She bristled, tensing up all over again. "I don't—"

He didn't get a chance to find out what she was going to say because James groaned deeply from the back of the wagon, followed by a weak, "Evangeline..."

She pierced Leo with a look before handing over the reins to climb into the back.

He was left holding a sleeping tot and staring over the oxen's ears, wondering what Evangeline would've said.

Eleven

EVANGELINE WOKE to bright sunlight streaming through the canvas tent, and a sense of wrongness stole over her.

She blinked against the light burning her eyes and registered the sounds of voices, something metal hitting metal—a cookpot?—and the far-off low of a cow.

She'd overslept, judging by how bright it was and how noisy the camp was. What time was it?

She yawned and reached her right arm out, intending to wake Sara. The girl usually rose early and nudged Evangeline until she woke up, too. Had she been as bone-tired as her mother?

Her hand encountered empty blankets.

Suddenly wide awake, Evangeline sat up. A glance around the interior of the tent showed it was empty.

"Sara?"

The memory of her daughter's tiny body being swept away in the creek surfaced even as Evangeline pulled on her boots and quickly checked that her dress was buttoned, that nothing had come undone while she slept.

She knew her hair was wild, down around her shoulders after coming loose during the night. But she didn't have time to deal with it, not if Sara had wandered off.

She pushed the tent flap open and stumbled out into the bright, mid-morning sunshine.

And found herself nearly on top of Leo's family. She didn't remember pitching her tent so close to their cookfire, but there it was. Someone had made a makeshift ring around the blaze with two barrels, a crate, and a saddle. Collin was standing over the pot on the fire while Coop lounged with his back against the saddle, a piece of grass between his lips. Alice was reading a book—one of Evangeline's novels—with a coffee tin in her other hand.

And there was Sara, sitting beside Leo, using a wooden box as a table. She had a tin fork clutched in her hand and some kind of red jam smeared at the side of her lip.

"Sissy!" she exclaimed gleefully when she caught sight of Evangeline.

Whose heart was still pounding with terror that she'd lost her little girl again. She pressed one hand against her sternum and could feel the slamming of that muscle.

Leo's intent gaze came to rest on her. He'd seen her at her worst already, but she became aware of her disheveled appearance, her hair down around her shoulders, how very behind she was.

She turned her back, taking two steps toward the tent. She kept her eyes on the tent pole as she reached up to quickly plait her hair. She heard the murmur of his voice behind her and then footsteps.

She didn't look at him as he approached. "It won't take me a minute to break down the tent," she said with a false smile. "I'm sorry I overslept." *Thank you for watching Sara.* She couldn't say the words or he'd see how very shaken she was. What kind of mother was she if she had slept through Sara leaving the tent?

When it came, his voice was gruff. "Hollis called for a rest day, remember? You don't have to take down the tent at all."

Now she glanced at him, saw the way he stared at her hands, where she had pulled the end of her braid over her shoulder and was lacing the last of the long tresses into a thick braid.

He was standing close. If she breathed too deeply, his scent would fill her nostrils. Leather and a horse and, beneath it all, something uniquely Leo. His scent had been stuck in her nostrils for hours after he'd given her a first lesson at driving the team. Every time she'd caught a whiff of him after that, she'd felt anew the way his shoulder had pressed into hers, the way her elbow would brush his side as the wagon rocked them together.

She broke off the stare they both seemed to be caught in and her sluggish brain finally caught up with his earlier words.

A rest day. She did remember that. It suddenly made sense why Leo's brothers were lounging around the fire, why they hadn't broken camp yet. The recollection had gotten lost in the rush of worry over Sara's whereabouts and Evangeline's exhaustion from sitting up late into the night with Father.

Leo cleared his throat. She didn't dare look him in the face again. She sensed him look over her head, his attention in the far distance.

"I should go check on Father," she murmured. Anything for a little space.

It'd been three days since their deal had been struck. Three days of being closer to Leo than she wanted, of Father in pain and ill. His fever had worsened yesterday. When he was awake, he was groggy and confused. Asleep, he murmured nonsense and thrashed his head on the pillow.

"How late were you up with him last night?" Leo's voice didn't sound quite right, but she couldn't begin to guess why.

She shook her head. Late. The campfires in the circle of wagons had been dying out. That's all she remembered before she'd crawled into the tent and fallen asleep.

She didn't know how to help Father. If they'd been back home, she would've called for a doctor. But there was no doctor here.

"Maddie made a new poultice and is sitting with him for a bit. Come and eat something."

No taking the tent down. Maddie was watching over father. No immediate chores. She didn't know what else to do, so she trailed Leo to the cookfire.

When she headed to the fire to make a plate, Leo gently pushed her toward the seat he'd abandoned. He fetched her a tin of coffee and a plate of Dutch-oven biscuits slathered with white gravy.

As she took the plate from his hands, she caught sight of Collin, sitting on the opposite side of the fire. His lips twitched with a suppressed smile.

"Coop usually calls *me* a mother hen," Alice said from behind her book. "I must've rubbed off on Leo. Or maybe you bring out that quality in him, Evangeline."

The attention flustered Evangeline, but before embarrassment completely overwhelmed her, Collin spoke from behind his coffee tin.

"He might've been called that—or worse—a few times at the mill." Collin and Coop exchanged a speaking glance.

"If someone came to work sick, he sent them home," Coop said with only a little hesitation. "And then usually sent Alice after them with a pot of soup."

Leo sat down beside Evangeline, a fresh cup of coffee in his hand wafting steam. "You two keep quiet."

Evangeline leaned past him to see Collin. "Don't listen to him. This is very enlightening. He's always been this protective?"

Alice put down her book, her eyes dancing. "When we were small, he'd have us trail him to the schoolhouse like little ducklings."

"If we got outta line, he got so mad." Coop chuckled to himself.

"Remember that one time," Collin interrupted. "That tall kid—what was his name?"

"Terrence Rogers," Alice supplied.

Leo only shook his head, hiding behind his coffee tin, his face filled with color.

She couldn't stop smiling at the way his siblings teased him.

"That's right," Collin went on. "He'd been picking on Coop for several days and then Leo went and had *a talk* with him after the dismissal bell."

Coop grinned, and even Alice was giggling now.

"I thought Terrence was going to wet his pants," Alice said through her laughter.

Leo shook his head and sighed. "Please don't listen to them."

She was opening her mouth to ask what had happened next when Father moaned loud enough to be heard through their chatter.

Suddenly, Evangeline's appetite disappeared. What was she doing? Enjoying herself while Father suffered? Coming West had been her idea, which meant his injury and this sickness was her fault. She shouldn't be having fun while he was in such misery.

She stood and handed her plate to Leo. "I'd better go check on him."

Leo's eyes were warm and compassionate. "Do you want me to go with you?"

"No. No, that's all right."

When Leo looked at her, he saw too much. And she couldn't afford to get too close to the man. Or his family.

No matter how much she wanted to be a part of their camaraderie.

* * *

After breakfast, Leo went to check on the cattle.

"You should wash up before worship!" Alice called after him.

He raised one hand in acknowledgement and didn't look back.

Sunday worship on a Monday. He'd heard plenty of chatter about it this morning in camp. No one seemed to care that it was Monday, they were relieved for the rest day and looking forward to worshiping together.

The cattle were fine, lazying around in the cool morning air.

He met Collin at the creek. His brother shook off his wet hair like a dog, spraying droplets in the air.

He tossed the bar of lye soap to Leo. "Better clean up before your sweetheart gets too close."

Leo pulled a face at him.

Collin smirked but left him to the washing up.

He'd needed to dunk his head in the cold water after the scene back at the campfire. Not his siblings' teasing. He was used to that.

Seeing Evangeline with her hair down, flustered because she'd overslept, her eyes shaded with a hint of vulnerability... It'd hit him like a kick in the gut. She was so beautiful. Far more beautiful than the likes of him should even be close to.

He made quick work of scrubbing his face and hands in the icy creek water. He was still shivering with cold when he approached the ring of wagons.

Alice and Evangeline and Sara were standing near his family's wagon. Evangeline was smiling at something Alice must've said, but when she turned to glance at him, it felt like her smile was meant for him.

He almost stumbled over his own feet.

If he'd thought her pretty in her sleep-rumpled state, this was something else. She had put on a different dress, this one a sky blue that made her eyes shine. She had done something with her hair, pulling it back in an intricate design. He didn't know the name for it, he just knew that it made her look as fine as a fancy piece of china. Something to look at but not touch.

He wished he had had some other clothes to put on. Wash day wasn't for another two days.

Collin cuffed him on the shoulder, startling him and making him realize he had stopped cold to stare. "She's a pretty sight, ain't she?"

His brother's words were a poke. He should've told Evangeline she looked beautiful instead of staring at her like a dolt.

She'd already glanced away, a faint flush rising in her cheeks.

He'd lost his chance.

And then Owen and August walked around the wagon.

"Who invited them," Leo mumbled.

"Alice," Collin said.

Alice.

Both brothers had added a dark vest over their shirt, fancying up their outfit. Leo recognized the trousers as their everyday pants, but they had brushed their hats and, once again, Leo wished he could've been something different.

Owen sidled right up to Evangeline. "You look as beautiful as a wild rose. Care to walk over to the gathering with me?"

Evangeline blushed prettily. Leo swallowed back resentment that he hadn't given a compliment. He stepped forward, his arm reaching out, but he didn't know his own mind, whether he meant to grab her around the waist or prevent Owen from getting any closer.

"Why don't we all walk over together?" Alice played peacemaker.

Evangeline tucked her arm through the crook of Leo's elbow as if it was the most natural thing to do. As if that had been his intention all along.

He couldn't help the way his chest puffed out when Owen's eyes locked on their connection.

Around them, everyone seemed to be in good spirits,

calling out greetings as they walked to the little clearing on the edge of camp. Most everyone had a crate or barrel in hand to sit on.

They were halfway there when Leo realized that Coop wasn't with them. He made as if to turn around, but Alice shook her head slightly. "He didn't want to come."

The man didn't need to skip a chance to listen to the Word. But if Leo lectured him, Coop would stay away out of spite.

Evangeline settled on a crate. Sara crawled into her lap, clutching a rag doll. Leo stood slightly behind her.

A male voice from the front of the crowd led a rousing rendition of "Come, Christians, Join to Sing" and of course Evangeline would have the most beautiful soprano voice he'd ever heard.

He couldn't carry much of a tune and sang softly so he wouldn't ruin the singing for her.

Sometime over the past two days, he had stopped thinking of her as a spoiled society miss. She wasn't that. He didn't know why she had a hard time trusting folks, but she'd folded into his family easily enough.

Sara climbed off of her lap and toddled over to Owen. She lifted the doll for him to see. Leo was glad that the man looked exceedingly foolish as he played dolly with the little girl.

The song changed to "Amazing Grace," and Evangeline's voice stuttered as the words lifted around them.

Her face turned downcast, then, all of a sudden, she stood up. She pressed one hand on his shoulder and slipped away in the direction that they had come. He exchanged a concerned glance with Alice, who quickly whispered that she would watch over Sara. He followed Evangeline as she skirted the circled wagons.

Had singing that song upset her? Or was it something else?

She disappeared between their two wagons. He drew up short, still half-hidden, when he saw her talking to Coop near the campfire.

"A little too much piety for you?" Coop asked.

"No." Evangeline didn't give any more of an answer than that. She had her hands folded in front of her waist and stared at the fire. "What about you?"

"Folks like them don't understand folks like me."

"Them?"

"Everybody over at that Sunday meeting."

"Not even your brother? Alice?"

Coop laughed, a bitter sound. "Leo understands me the least. He wants me to be something I'm not."

Evangeline was silent, but Coop went on.

"I've made some mistakes. Leo can't see past them."

Leo faded behind the wagon, further out of sight.

Some mistakes. Was that how Coop saw it? Leo and Alice and Collin had had to uproot their entire lives because of Coop's mistakes.

And Coop didn't seem to want to change his ways. Leo didn't know how to reach him. He didn't want Evangeline feeling sorry for his brother, but before he could make a move and interrupt them, Evangeline said softly, "I've made mistakes, too."

Coop's curious, intent stare landed on her. "Maybe my brother will be more forgiving of yours." He lifted his coffee to salute her.

Leo saw the way her expression settled into resigned lines. Was she thinking about how things between them were only pretend? They were playacting. He didn't need to forgive her for anything.

She slipped away to her wagon, probably to check on her father. But not before Leo caught a glimpse of sadness written on her face.

What caused it?

It wasn't his business. He didn't even know whether she would call him a friend. But all of a sudden, he wanted to know. He wanted to comfort her, reassure her.

Not that it was his place.

Twelve

"YOU THINK THERE'S ANYTHING... strange about Fairfax?" Collin asked.

Collin and Coop were saddling up, and Collin couldn't help his gaze straying to where Fairfax was hefting a saddle onto that monster he called a horse. A couple of men scouting ahead had seen a herd of deer grazing. Hollis had called for an early halt and several of the men from camp were going on a hunt, hoping to bring down a buck large enough to feed several families.

"He's a weakling," Coop said without looking up from his cinch.

"Other than that."

Stephen had barely been able to hitch his oxen when the journey had begun. Now he did so capably and quickly, even though he was so short he could barely see over the animals' shoulders.

"What d'you mean?" Coop patted his horse and moved the bridle to rest on the saddle, ready for him to sit in it.

Collin slid his rifle into a scabbard on his own saddle.

What *did* he mean?

"You can't tell anyone."

"*I'm tired of hiding in the wagon all the time. I want to go back to normal.*"

"*It's not safe.*"

The memory of the conversation he'd overheard played in his mind and curiosity surged all over again, just like it had every time he'd thought of those moments over the past three days. It'd been bedtime, everyone settling in for the night. He'd left the circle of wagons to take a leak and had been slipping back through camp. He happened to come in right by the Fairfax wagon. He didn't know whose voices he'd overheard, but the conversation had stuck with him.

It's not safe. There were plenty of dangers on this journey. Getting snakebit, getting trampled, getting shot by some greenhorn who shouldn't be wielding a weapon.

But he had the sense that whoever had been talking in that wagon—Stephen maybe?—hadn't been talking about any of that. *I'm tired of hiding.*

What were the Fairfaxes hiding from?

Collin shook his head to clear the thoughts. Coop was still waiting on his answer. *What d'you mean?*

"Like... his mannerisms. His smile." Or lack of one.

Stephen rarely smiled. He was one of the most serious young men Collin had ever met. But every once in awhile, when he was with his sisters, he'd smile. It made his face look almost... pretty. "Have you ever seen him with more than a day's shadow of whiskers on his chin?"

Coop stepped into the stirrup and eased into his saddle with a creak of leather. He shot a cutting glance at Collin. "His smile? You're noticing his smile? You don't think there's something strange about that?"

Collin had endured Coop's teasing since they were young boys. He teased his brother mercilessly. But this wasn't a joking matter.

"I'm not joshing around."

Coop read his seriousness. He could see it in his twin's

eyes. But Coop shook his head. "Lotta men don't grow whiskers that young. I put him what... nineteen? Twenty?"

Collin knew that. It wasn't only the whiskers that bugged him.

"'Sides, you didn't grow any whiskers until just last year."

Coop urged his horse into a canter and all Collin heard was his hearty laugh as he rode off.

Collin shook his head as he checked the saddle once more. How long had it been since Coop had given him a hard time like that? Months, maybe.

Was it only because Leo wasn't around? Over the past week, Leo had been busy as a bee helping Evangeline with whatever she needed. Driving her wagon. Kissing her goodnight. At least, he hoped that's what Leo was doing when he went walking with her in the evenings. Maybe Leo would lighten up on Coop if he had his own family to worry about.

Collin stepped into his saddle and adjusted his seat. He wasn't going to be deterred from his suspicions just because Coop thought he was ridiculous.

A group of men congregated on horseback just outside the circle of wagons. And there was Stephen, still saddling up. Was he... talking to his horse? Collin couldn't be sure from this distance, but it sure looked like the man was scolding his animal.

The horse was opposite the man in every way. Seventeen hands tall, black as night compared to Stephen's fair complexion, and as spirited as they came.

Collin guided his horse toward the gathering group, trying to put his mind on something else. There were plenty of other things to worry about, including staying safe in a hunting party that included city men who didn't know one end of a rifle from another.

But he couldn't stop thinking about Stephen. If the Fairfaxes were frightened, someone should help. And Stephen would never ask. The man kept to himself. The whole family did, sticking close to their wagon, never sharing a meal with other families. Collin had initially thought them standoffish, but what if they were just scared?

It didn't sit right with Collin. Maybe he should befriend Stephen, try to get him to open up.

"Stephen, ride along with me and Coop," he called.

For a moment, it looked like Stephen wanted to argue. But then the young man wheeled his mount and the three of them went south while the other groups dispersed.

"One of the scouts said there's a little gully that cuts along the plain not far ahead." Coop pointed.

Collin nodded, and they headed that way.

Stephen's horse danced underneath him, almost managing to unseat him.

"You all right?" Collin asked.

"Fine," came the terse answer.

"He's a lot of horse," Coop said. "You ever think about trading him for something more manageable?"

"No."

An awkward silence ensued.

Collin tried to break it. "You work back home?"

Stephen grunted. "In a factory. Since I was fifteen."

"Powder mill for me and my brothers. Sure is different out here."

Stephen went silent again. How was Collin supposed to make friends with him when the man didn't seem to want to talk at all?

They went quiet after that, knowing that their voices carried and could scare off any game. They spread out slightly, several yards in between each horse as they meandered toward the gully, eyes peeled for something to shoot.

Almost an hour passed. Collin was beginning to think of this as a lost cause when Coop made a motion with his hand. Collin sent a signal to Stephen even as he scanned the horizon for whatever Coop had seen.

There it was. A buck with a nice rack of antlers grazing thirty yards away.

He drew in; saw Stephen do the same, from the corner of his eye. They were downwind. The animal hadn't noticed them yet.

Coop drew his weapon and carefully balanced the rifle. His shot rang out and the buck fell.

"Good shot," he called to his brother.

The trio started walking their horses toward the fallen buck. Collin was on alert to see if the buck would rise again.

"You ever skin a deer?" Collin asked Stephen as they converged on the carcass.

The man shook his head.

The three dismounted and carefully approached. Coop's shot had been sure. The buck was dead.

Coop rolled his eyes at Collin when Stephen wasn't looking, but he unsheathed his skinning knife and extended it, handle outward, toward Stephen. "You want to do the honors?"

Alice would've begged off. She didn't like butchering, not even chickens.

Stephen firmed his lips and followed Coop's directions to slice through the deer's skin, letting the blood flow into the grass.

He was deathly pale, hand shaking, but didn't shirk from any of it. He finished the job with quick strokes and handed the knife back to Coop.

Then he stood up, turned away, and vomited into the grass.

Collin stared. He hadn't expected that.

Stephen wiped his mouth with the back of his hand. "We ready to go?"

* * *

"Come on. We're going on an adventure." Leo leaned around the edge of the wagon where Evangeline was sorting through a stack of books in a crate. Sara was at her feet, playing with a wooden ball.

Evangeline creased her brows. "Didn't you go hunting with the other men?"

"Not this time. There's plenty of them to bring back some game. And I had another idea. Come with me."

She glanced toward the wagon bed. He'd anticipated that she wouldn't want to leave her father.

"Irene said she would sit with him for a little while. It will do you good to stretch your legs."

This time she raised her brows at him. "Isn't that what we've been doing every day?"

He grinned. "I promise I won't make you walk far."

He could see she was curious from the way she glanced back into the wagon. She thought she had to stay with her father at all hours.

He squatted down next to Sara. "Don't you want to come have some fun? Tell sissy you want to go on an adventure."

Maybe it was underhanded, but the girl turned her sweet eyes onto Evangeline, who gave an exasperated sigh.

"Just for a little while," she said.

"Of course."

Leo led them toward the creek. They'd been driving the wagons parallel to it all day. He knew there would be places ahead where water was scarce, and this was an opportunity he couldn't pass up. It was cool and peaceful beneath the trees that lined the snaking water. Sunlight filtered through the canopy above, and squirrels rustled in the branches overhead.

It didn't take long to find a perfect spot. He stopped walking, waiting for Evangeline and Sara, who were dawdling behind him, to catch up.

"Here we are," he said.

Evangeline glanced around dubiously. "This is the place for an adventure?"

"Sure it is. Have you ever been fishing before?"

She scrunched up her nose, and it was adorable. "No, I've never been fishing."

"I bet you've read about it."

She shot him a pointed look and he couldn't help smiling. "I'm right, aren't I?"

"I might have read one or two stories where fishing played a very minor part." Said with her nose tilted up in the air.

"I bet you've read more than that. I bet you can tell me the best place to fish for trout. Even what I should use for bait."

She pursed her lips and turned her head like she didn't want to answer him. But then she burst out, "You've picked the right spot. That little pool behind the eddy, where the water is quiet, *should* be where the fish are. And there are a lot of types of bait you could use. It mostly depends on whether they are hungry."

He grinned at her, finally earning her lopsided smile. He extended the slender line with a small hook he'd carved out of a chunk of firewood last night. He'd bribed a little boy from another wagon to dig him up two earthworms, and he'd hooked one of the wriggly things. He'd tied the other end of the line to a sturdy stick about a foot long and an inch wide.

"You should put it in there. Experience fishing for yourself, not from the pages you've read."

She only hesitated for a moment.

He showed her how to drop the line into the water, explained what the tug on the line might feel like if a fish took the bait and hook.

And then, when she was holding the line in her arms, looking uncertain, he backed up a few steps and reached out his hand for Sara. "Do you think we could find some tadpoles? Let's go look."

Evangeline threw a glance of wide-eyed panic at him. "You can't just leave me here."

"We aren't going far. We don't want to scare off the fish

you're gonna catch for our lunch." And he had a hunch Sara was going to be wading in the water before too long.

"But—"

He hid his smile with a turn of his head. "It'll be all right, even if it doesn't go perfectly the first time."

She still didn't look convinced, but she didn't argue again as he followed Sara a few feet down the bank of the creek. The girl seemed amazed by everything. A shiny rock. A snail. A twig shaped like a Y.

Evangeline relaxed when she realized he wasn't going to leave her to fend for herself.

A bird with gray plumage and white and black on its tail landed in the branches a dozen feet above his head. Sara craned her neck, trying to see it.

"See the bird," she said.

"Did your sister tell you what kind of bird that one is?"

Evangeline was still within earshot. "It's a mockingbird," she said.

Of course she would know. "I bet you can tell me every kind of fish to be found in this stream, too."

Was she blushing? He couldn't tell in the dappled sunlight throwing shadows on her face. "I don't—I don't intend to come off as a know-it-all. I knew this journey would be difficult, so I read as much as I could to prepare."

"I don't think you're a know-it-all."

She looked surprised.

Maybe he had thought that at first, when she had been shoving her trail guides in his face. But now that he knew her better, he saw that if she wasn't certain, she tried to find the answer in a book.

"How come you like to read so much?" he asked.

Sara was at his feet, squatting on the creek bank and dipping her fingers into the water.

Evangeline focused on the water in front of her, and it gave him a chance to watch her. "My mother passed away when I was very small. I was always taken care of. There were nannies and tutors. But my father spent most of his time working. Books kept me entertained. They were... friends, in a sense."

"Tutors. Not school?"

She shook her head. "Not school."

It was so different from his own experience that he had a hard time fathoming it.

"Did you read a lot when you were younger?" she asked.

The question was meant innocently, but he didn't want to say it. *I can't read.* Someone as smart as Evangeline would eventually end up with a man who was a match for her intelligence.

He stretched his lips into the semblance of a smile. "I mostly got into scrapes. Or tried to keep my brothers out of them."

She made a humming sound. "Not Alice?"

"No. Not Alice." At least, not when they had been children. Braddock was still present on the wagon train, stubbornly traveling west when Leo had expected him to turn back soon after the journey started. Back in New Jersey, Alice had interacted with him much more than any of her brothers —he'd rarely visited the powder mill.

His presence made Leo itchy. What did he want with Alice?

Before he could say anything else, she startled, nearly dropping the line. "I think something—something pulled on the line!"

"Pull back," he said.

He left Sara digging in the mud with a stick she'd found and went to Evangeline, who was almost dancing on the bank.

"Pull it out of the water," he said over a chuckle.

She yanked on the string, far too hard, but a beautiful perch plunked out onto the bank. It flopped toward her feet. She shrieked a little, and this time he couldn't stop a hearty laugh. He grabbed hold of the line before the fish could hop back into the water, gripping its lip and lifting it so she could see.

"This'll make a nice little lunch for us," he said.

Sara had dropped her stick and now stood beside him. She watched with wide eyes.

"You want to hold it?" Leo asked Evangeline.

He expected her to dance away again, but she surprised him by stepping closer. "All right."

He showed her how to grip with her thumb inside the fish's lip. And then he dropped the fish in her hands.

She shuddered. "I caught this."

He found himself standing too close. When she looked up at him, pride and happiness sparkled up out of her eyes. He was drawn to her—couldn't help shifting infinitesimally closer.

He knew it wasn't part of their deal, but he couldn't keep his gaze from falling to her lips.

She seemed to be caught in the same undercurrent of attraction that he was, her eyes widening slightly as she realized it.

All he would have to do was lean forward, tip her chin up...

"I wanna touch!" Sara pulled on his pant leg, breaking the fine tension that hung in the air.

He sucked in a breath, not realizing until just this moment that he'd been holding it.

Evangeline was already bent over, showing her prize to her sister.

He took off his hat, ran his hand through his hair. What was that?

He'd been too caught up in the moment, that's what. They'd both shared a little about their childhoods. What was between them was starting to feel like friendship.

But it wasn't. He had to remember he was the hired help. Just like the tutors she'd told him about.

Thirteen

THE NEXT EVENING, Evangeline sat with her father near the wagon, helping him eat his supper.

She lifted the spoon toward his mouth, saw his frown, saw in his eyes how much he disliked this.

He lifted his arm to intercept her hand, but the movement must've pulled his ribs because he hissed in a breath.

He dropped his hand to his side. She tipped the spoonful of broth into his mouth.

She looked away, not really seeing the camp around them but knowing her father well enough to know he wouldn't want her to see his pain.

She'd been grateful that his fever had gone down sometime during the day, while Leo had been driving the wagon. Father had felt well enough to ask Leo to help him go for a walk.

She'd felt something shift and soften inside her as she'd watched Leo lead her father away with one hand around his back to steady him.

Leo was...

She didn't know what he was, but he certainly made her

feel things she didn't want to feel. Like yesterday on the banks of that winding creek, when they'd been standing too close together. His eyes had fallen to her lips and she'd felt a visceral pull inside.

She'd wanted his kiss.

What a disaster.

She couldn't trust herself.

The last person she'd kissed had been Jeremy. And he'd betrayed her. She didn't want to be drawn to Leo. Didn't want to want anyone, ever again.

She'd still been so discomfited by the near-kiss from yesterday that when Hollis had called a halt for the day, she'd gone straight to work.

She'd stripped Father's makeshift bed in the wagon and quickly washed out the sweat-soiled blankets in the creek.

When she'd returned to camp, she'd found that Leo had rigged her father a seat against the side of the wagon using a couple of crates lashed together. Father could rest his back— and his ribs—against the wagon. He'd been quiet, with white lines of pain bracketing his mouth, but he hadn't asked to lie down as she'd hung the blankets to dry as best she could.

Leo had made all of it possible.

As if her thoughts had conjured him, Leo appeared from around his family's wagon. Sara trailed him, both of them carrying an armload of wood. Sara's was noticeably smaller, but she glanced up at the man with pride shining on her face.

He made sure she didn't get too close to Alice's cookfire as they stacked the wood. He glanced in Evangeline's direction. She quickly averted her gaze.

"He's a good sort," Father mumbled the words just before she raised the spoon to his lips again.

Evangeline made a non-committal hum.

"Good with Sara," Father said after he'd swallowed.

There was no denying that. When Evangeline had refused Leo's help putting up the tent, Sara had followed him around the campsite, chattering the entire time.

He was patient with her. Maybe more patient than Evangeline after a long day of walking.

Father ate another couple of bites in silence while Evangeline ignored Leo completely.

"You don't like him?" Father finally asked. Thank goodness his words were pitched low enough that Leo wouldn't overhear.

"I like him fine," she said, though she couldn't meet Father's eyes as she raised the spoon. "I hired him to help us, didn't I?"

"I forgot about that."

She'd told her father about the deal in whispers, that first day after his ordeal. She had wanted him to rest easy, knowing things would be all right until he was on his feet again.

She couldn't have kept on without Leo's help. But she also hadn't expected it to be so difficult to have him near.

Jeremy had charmed her from the beginning. He'd said all the right things, convinced her to spend more and more time with him, had pushed for the intimacy she'd known she shouldn't give in to. And then she'd found out she was with child only days before she'd discovered his infidelity.

As much as she could tell, Leo was nothing like Jeremy.

She'd made the deal from the start because of it. Leo wasn't afraid of hard work, he was stubborn and bossy. She'd thought the moments of attraction when he'd pulled her from the creek were an aberration. A moment of relief at being rescued.

But something had changed between them over the past weeks.

She couldn't name it, but it was there in the soft way he looked at her.

And she couldn't allow herself to trust in it.

After Father was finished eating, she made up a bed in his own tent and helped him settle in for the night. He was still weak, and by the time she backed out of his tent, her own emotions were out of control.

She still had to get Sara ready for bed. The girl could be an ordeal when she was exhausted. All Evangeline wanted to do was crawl in her own bedroll and close her eyes.

Where was Sara? Her heart pattered in her chest before she heard the low, even tones of Leo's voice. Where...?

She caught sight of his broad shoulders where he sat half-hidden just outside the open tent flap, not far away. Her feet carried her in that direction. Sara was inside, lying on her bedroll with her head tipped up, listening.

"The little lamb walked and walked, but he couldn't find his mama..."

He was telling a bedtime story, Evangeline realized.

Sara was already in her nightgown and looked peaceful and drowsy.

When Evangeline would've approached, Leo nodded toward the pot of coffee still on the fire. A moment of freedom? Time just for herself?

She wanted it desperately.

But Leo had done so much for her already. She feared she owed him much more than the price she'd agreed to pay.

She feared she was starting to admire him.

She didn't dare let herself do anything that would open her heart more.

So she turned her feet toward the tent.

Leo saw her intention and leaned into the tent to say something. He straightened to his full height as Evangeline neared.

"Alice took her to wash up at the creek after supper," he whispered. "And helped her get ready for bed."

"Thank you for taking care of her." She didn't dare look at him, instead focusing on a spot over his shoulder.

"Your father seemed better tonight," he whispered.

She nodded.

He touched her wrist, just a brush of his fingertips, but the contact shocked her so that she forgot her resolve not to look at him. His gaze was almost unreadable in the growing dark. "You all right?"

"I'm fine."

She slipped into the tent, not looking back as she quickly tied off the flap.

She crawled into her bed, but there was no settling as her heart was pounding nearly out of her chest.

This was trouble.

Because Leo made her feel safe. She wanted to sink into his arms.

She couldn't trust that feeling.

And she couldn't forget that she was keeping a secret. The secret of Sara's parentage. If Leo found out, he'd think she had loose morals. Why would he want a woman like that?

He wouldn't.

She'd never tell her secret. Not when a new start for Sara depended on it.

* * *

Leo sat next to the cookfire that was mostly ash and a few glowing embers. Dawn was breaking, but most of the camp slept on. Small spires of smoke rose into the sky. Snores emanated from some of the wagons. The horses were picketed not far off, and some were up and grazing from the dewy grass.

He'd stoke the fire here in a bit, so it'd be ready for Alice.

He couldn't stop thinking about Evangeline. He'd caught the flash of what looked like trepidation in her expression last night just before she'd scurried inside her tent, as if she couldn't get away from him fast enough.

She'd put her walls up.

He saw it in the way she interacted with her father. She loved the man, clearly. She'd stayed up late into the night with him, several nights in a row, putting damp rags on his head to keep his fever down.

Leo had watched her last night as she'd helped the man eat his dinner. She held herself apart, held something back.

The question was, why?

Leo wasn't an expert on relationships, but it bugged him. If she couldn't open up to her father, who could she talk to?

Was the rift between them the same reason she kept putting distance between herself and Leo?

Coop wandered past the tent where Collin and Alice were sleeping. He'd been on the last watch and now he yawned so big that his jaw cracked.

He caught sight of Leo, but his relaxed posture didn't change. "Mornin'," he mumbled.

Leo had put a pot of coffee on the embers he'd stirred up. Coop helped himself to a cup.

The silence stretched between them. Leo remembered those moments with Evangeline and Sara on the creek bank, remembered thinking for a fleeting moment how he missed those times with Coop, when they'd been young and able to play together.

"Your horse came up lame yesterday afternoon. I took a stone out of his hoof. Thought you'd want to know."

"Thanks." Leo was surprised. Maybe he shouldn't be. Coop had always had an affinity for animals.

Coop sipped his coffee. "You asked Evangeline to marry you yet?"

He frowned at his brother's unexpected, impertinent question. "No, and I'll thank you to stay out of my business."

He couldn't tell Coop that things weren't like that for him and Evangeline. She'd marry someone. Probably in Oregon. But she'd made it real clear that it wouldn't be Leo.

He thought about that almost-kiss. What if she *did* like him?

He almost got lost in his thoughts of Evangeline. Almost didn't notice the fancy silver pocket watch that Coop used to casually check the time.

"What's that?" he asked as Coop slipped the watch back into his pocket, leaving a fine chain hanging down.

"Nothing."

"Didn't look like nothing." He stood up. The fire was still between him and his brother.

Coop's chin jerked at a stubborn angle. "I won it."

When was this? Why hadn't Collin said anything? Had he known?

"How'd you win it?"

Coop's eyes glittered. "That's my business."

"Playing cards?" Leo spat. "You—"

Coop tossed his coffee tin into the dirt. "Stay outta it."

Leo stood and watched in disbelief as his brother stalked off. He had half a mind to go after him. To shake him and make him spill everything. Where and when was he playing cards? Was he drinking again?

A frustrated growl rose in Leo's throat, but he swallowed it back.

"Everything all right?"

Leo's hackles went up. Of course it would be Owen's voice from only a few feet away. He'd probably heard everything.

"Go away." Suddenly exhausted, Leo didn't have it in him to make nice with his half brother today.

But Owen didn't listen. He had his own cup of coffee and moved to stand next to Leo, both of them looking into the sunrise.

Fine. Didn't mean Leo had to talk to him.

"I didn't know about you," Owen said mildly, as if they were having a friendly conversation. "Didn't know I had another brother until Pa was on his deathbed and he told me 'n August."

"I don't care." Leo didn't want to think about the father who'd abandoned him and Alice. The man had walked away, divorced their mother, and never looked back.

"I care. I was so angry at him for months after he passed."

Leo didn't want to feel a sense of camaraderie, not with Owen. "So what?" he ground out. "You want some kind of award or something?"

There was a part of him that knew it wasn't fair. It wasn't Owen who'd abandoned him. It was his father.

But Owen was all wrapped up in it, and fair or not, Leo didn't want another brother.

"I know you don't want anything to do with me, but I can help you."

Leo's temper spiked. He turned on Owen.

The other man didn't back down, faced Leo on the balls of his toes. "You got your hands full helping out the pretty Evangeline. Seems like you could use an extra pair of eyes around camp. Or two."

Leo's breath caught. He went still, the nervous energy coursing through him abating. Was Owen saying...?

"August and I can keep an eye out. If Coop's getting into trouble—"

"You come to me." It wasn't a question. Leo hadn't even intended to say the words, but they came out a demand. "Coop's my blood. I'll be the one who takes responsibility for him."

Owen's gaze shuttered. He didn't say anything about being Leo's blood, too. Maybe he knew Leo wouldn't have been able to stand it.

"What'll this help cost me?" Leo asked.

Owen considered it. "It'd be nice to eat one of Alice's meals. All together." Like a family.

He didn't say it, but Leo heard it loud and clear.

He thought about refusing. Owen knew about Coop getting into trouble on the trail but not what'd happened back home. Braddock was still present, still nosing around.

Being around Owen and August meant he'd need Alice and Collin and Coop to keep their traps shut about New Jersey. He didn't want any of that following them to Oregon.

But he did need help. There wasn't enough of him to go around. He didn't want it to be Owen, but what choice did he have?

"Fine," he said

"Fine," Owen echoed.

Fourteen

LEO HAD SEEMED LIGHTER over the next two days, Evangeline reflected. His smiles came easier, and he was more relaxed, though still watchful.

Father was improving. It was slow, to be sure, but he was definitely getting better. His fever had gone, but there were still days he was so weak he couldn't walk beside the wagon, and his cough remained.

Evangeline couldn't forget the disappointment in his expression when she'd confided that her relationship with Leo was only a business deal. It was unexpected, that was all. She'd thought Father would be relieved, knowing that she wouldn't make the same mistakes all over again.

Leo confused her. Yesterday, he and Sara had gone walking while she and Alice had prepared supper. When they'd returned, Sara had run to Evangeline and presented a posy of wildflowers tied with a bit of twine. Evangeline had exclaimed her delight over the flowers. Sara had preened. And behind her, Leo had smiled a slow smile, like the dawning of the sun.

Evangeline's stomach had flip-flopped in such a terrifying way that she'd had to excuse herself quickly after supper.

She'd spent half the night tossing and turning in her bedroll, remembering that smile.

She couldn't fancy Leo. She wouldn't allow herself.

Tonight, she was cooking supper for everyone in Alice's big cookpot. Alone.

She'd thought to give Alice a break. Alice, who looked after everyone. She cooked. She washed laundry. She darned socks and sewed on buttons. She even watered the horses and pitched the tent.

More than that, she and Collin played peacemaker between Leo and Coop. The oldest and youngest brothers were still circling each other warily, sometimes almost angrily.

Alice deserved a break. And after weeks of teaching Evangeline how to cook, she'd insisted Alice take the night off. Alice didn't use a cookbook. She'd memorized numerous recipes. Sometimes Evangeline wondered whether she just made them up on the spot.

Evangeline tried to recreate a stew they'd had only a few days ago, as best she could remember.

But as she stared into the pot, she felt a sense of foreboding. Coop had brought her an already-skinned rabbit that he'd taken during the day as he'd pushed the cattle. She'd made stew, just like Alice had showed her.

But her biscuits, made over the open fire, were flatter than Alice's had been. And more brown around the edges.

She was worried about how the stew would taste.

It was too late to do anything about it now. Here came Leo and Sara, their faces scrubbed as if they'd just washed up. Collin and Coop were just behind. And Owen and August came from the opposite direction, both with steaming plates in their hands. They'd recently taken to eating supper with the Masons, though Leo still kept his distance. Father joined last, coming around the wagon from the opposite direction.

"Mmm, rabbit stew." Coop rubbed his hands together in anticipation before he bent and grabbed a tin plate from the stack Evangeline had set out on a barrel near the fire.

As Coop ladled stew onto his plate, she could hear an audible gurgle from Collin's stomach, as he was standing the closest.

Her own stomach was knotted with nerves.

Coop shoved a spoonful into his mouth even before he walked away, but he'd turned, and Evangeline couldn't see his reaction.

Leo motioned for her to fill her plate before him as Collin moved away from the cooking pot.

Evangeline thought the stew smelled all right as she bent close to the pot, dishing out some for her and Sara to share.

She moved to a crate nearer her wagon and sat down, calling Sara over. Evangeline handed the girl a too-flat biscuit. She examined it suspiciously.

Leo was ladling his own stew when Alice marched around the curve of wagons, a tall, dark-haired man walking beside her. Robert Braddock. His shoulders were turned toward her.

But they seemed to be arguing. "We're friends."

Coop went rigid from his seat opposite. Owen watched Coop while Collin shook his head, mouth set in a tight line.

Arms akimbo, Alice turned away from the man. "We've never been friends," she threw the words over her shoulder and made her way past Owen, toward her supper.

"Do you want to walk some more?" The man called out to Alice.

"We weren't walking," she returned crossly.

Evangeline should look away, give her friend privacy. But she couldn't quite tear her eyes away. She'd never seen Alice cross. Not even when Collin had lost the button she'd sewn on just the day before.

The man looked uncertain, his gaze holding on Alice until it was clear she wasn't going to acknowledge him. His eyes darted around the campsite, landing on each of the men in turn, while a muscle ticked in his jaw. Then he turned and walked away.

Coop went back to his food, and Collin's shoulders relaxed as he exchanged a look with Leo.

"How did the stew turn out?" Alice asked brightly, as if the overheard argument had never happened.

Collin coughed into his hand. Coop stared at his plate, chewing for too long.

Evangeline took a bite. The flavor was wrong.

"It's good," Leo said. Obviously, the man was trying to spare her feelings.

Collin coughed again.

Alice took a bite as she stood over the pot. She shook her head at all of them. "For heaven's sake. It only needs some salt." She quickly moved to the back of the wagon, where the family kept a small barrel of salt. She brought it to the pot, and as she added a few pinches to the stew, Collin and Coop approached the fire. She added a smaller amount to their plates.

She looked over at Leo, who shook his head.

"I'm sorry." Evangeline's cheeks burned. She didn't like making mistakes, and she especially didn't like everyone knowing about them.

"It's good," Leo repeated.

"Yeah, it's fine," Collin said, eating at more of his normal clip now that the food was salted.

"Alice has burnt dinner more times than I can count," Coop grunted.

Alice seemed unfazed, moving to sit close to Evangeline. "I can burn your food tomorrow, if you'd like."

Owen laughed, and Alice lifted her chin in his direction.

Alice glanced at Evangeline. "You did a fine job. A little more practice and you'll be better than I am."

Alice was a good friend.

"Who was that?" Evangeline whispered. She nodded toward where the man had disappeared.

Alice shook her head. "No one." She sighed. "Rob Braddock. I—we knew him back in New Jersey. I worked as a maid for his grandfather, who owned the mill where my brothers worked."

"He's a dunce," Coop called out, obviously eavesdropping on their conversation.

Alice shook her head again. "I don't know why he joined this wagon train. His grandfather is the wealthiest man in New Jersey."

"And he's a dunce," Coop repeated.

"He can barely ride," Collin said to his plate.

"He can't control his team," Leo added, voice low. "Almost caused a crash with another wagon our second day out."

"He's a city-slicker," Alice said. "I'll be shocked if he makes it to Fort Kearny."

Fort Kearny would be the first major stop, not far over the Nebraska border.

"If he makes it to Oregon, you should marry him," Coop teased.

"Maybe I will," Alice quipped.

A shadow moved behind the neighboring wagon across the way. It was Braddock. Alice's brothers, facing away, didn't see him. But Alice must've, though she ducked her head, wearing a chagrined frown.

Braddock disappeared into the growing dark, and Alice was quiet and contemplative as she stared out into the night.

Coop was the first one finished, but before he could excuse himself, Owen said, "I heard a rumor y'all might play some music for us tonight."

* * *

Leo hadn't known what his half brother was going to suggest, but it was obvious from the grin on Alice's face that she had been a part of this. He growled as Collin got a little too excited and went to the wagon for his fiddle. He also brought Leo's mouth organ.

Sara clapped her hands. She obviously knew what the instruments meant because she seemed delighted.

And Evangeline... She looked at him in surprise. Maybe he was only imagining it, but he thought he detected admiration in her expression.

"You play?" she asked.

"A little. And nothing too exciting."

Evangeline turned in the other direction. "What do you play?" she asked Alice.

Alice was still eating, but said through a full mouth, "I don't."

Leo wouldn't leave her out. "She sings. Like a nightingale."

Alice rolled her eyes but smiled.

Leo didn't know what Braddock had wanted with Alice. He'd have to talk to his sister later. For now, he was relieved that Owen's idea for music would keep Coop at the campsite.

Suddenly, Owen revealed a guitar he'd hidden behind his seat.

Sara clapped her hands. "Guitar," she squealed.

And Evangeline was looking at Leo's half brother with a smile on her face.

Owen and Collin leaned their heads together. Seeing them like that, all friendly, turned Leo's stomach.

What was Owen's real motive for helping? Did that help come with strings?

Collin seemed unaware of Leo's frustration. He pulled the bow over the fiddle and a long note emerged. Owen strummed the guitar. For a moment, their melody was off, and Leo felt a twinge of satisfaction.

And then they fell easily into a raucous tune, one Leo happened to know. He caught Collin's raised brows and raised his mouth organ to his lips.

Sara started twirling near Evangeline, who was watching with delight written across her expressive face.

Several folks from nearby wagons stirred and began gathering around the campsite. Someone brought out another fiddle to join.

August stood and went to Evangeline. The firelight was flickering on her face, and she was smiling happily. He held out his hand. "Dance?"

"You don't play?" she asked.

August shook his head. "Not a musical bone in my body."

She took his hand and grabbed Sara with her other one. They moved away from the fire, and when Collin changed the tune to a lively jig, they began dancing.

Leo took too long to notice the change in tune and hit a jangle of off notes. He hid his frown behind his hands and the mouth organ.

Evangeline was a good dancer. She had an easy grace, and even though August had no sense of rhythm at all, she only smiled at him as if he was the best dancer she'd ever partnered.

Several other folks joined in. Sara reached up to her sister, clearly asking to be held. Evangeline accommodated her, lifting her into her arms and twirling her along with August.

Evangeline laughed. He couldn't hear it over the music, but he felt her shining joy like a physical touch. He missed a note, and Collin met his eyes from across the fire. Of course his brother noticed. Collin noticed everything.

The song changed again, and then again. Leo was almost dizzy with playing, but he wasn't going to stop, not if it kept Evangeline happy.

August somehow danced her over to him. "Let me take Sara for a bit. Dance with Evangeline."

Leo started to protest, but August already had the girl on his hip. "There's two extra fiddlers," he said. "No one will mind if you catch your breath for a bit."

Evangeline's eyes were dancing and Leo thought maybe he wouldn't catch his breath after all.

He slipped his mouth organ into his pocket and extended his hand. When her smaller hand rested in his palm, he felt the connection all the way down to his toes.

"I'm not a very good dancer." He wanted to set her expectations before anything else. She didn't seem to care as she tugged him forward. And then he was dancing with her. Her face was shining right up into his. Collin's fiddle went on a musical tangent, breaking from the other instruments in a dance all its own, the notes going faster and faster. Leo spun his partner in time with Collin's tune. This time, he was the reason she laughed. Then he looked into her face, and she stopped laughing.

Her breath seemed to catch as the moment stretched between them. He felt more dizzy than when he had been in the middle of the song. He missed a step and that seemed to break the invisible connection between them. She let go of him, and the joy on her face died a little.

She pressed the back of her hand to her forehead.

"I need to... I need a break."

He glanced over to where August still held Sara in his arms, doing a strange kind of galloping dance with a young lady Leo recognized from another wagon.

Evangeline must've followed his gaze because she allowed herself to be led out of the circle of light into the darkness beyond the wagon. The music was more muted here. She stood with her arms around her middle.

"I think we need to talk about our deal."

What did that mean?

"I know we said we would pretend, but the lines are getting blurred."

He stood in silence, trying to understand. "I don't know what that means. If you're asking whether I like you, the answer is yes."

She seemed to hold on more tightly to herself. "You can't."

He was too far away from her to touch her. Something told him that if he moved closer, she'd bolt. "I don't think there's much you can do to stop me. Unless you can stop being so likable."

"I'm not likable," she snapped. "I am obnoxious about my books. Stubborn. Independent."

"You're knowledgeable," he countered. "Persistent. Independent."

Someone must've moved out of the way because suddenly flickering firelight was thrown on her features and he saw her skeptical stare. "You can't use independent as a good quality when I used it as a bad one."

"Says who?"

She made a sound of frustration. He wanted her closer. Wanted to be back among the folks who were dancing, wanted to see her smiling up at him again. But there was also something inside that told him if he did or said the wrong thing at this moment, she might call off their whole deal. And then where would he be?

He had his family to think about.

"Stop distracting me," she said. "Father is better, though he's still not at full strength. I can drive the wagon. And—I think enough people have seen us together that if we tell them we don't suit, that we are only friends—"

"Why don't we suit?" He hadn't meant to blurt the words out. Not really. But he couldn't seem to stop now. "Because I'm not smart enough for you? Because I can't read?"

"You can't read?"

He scowled. "I figured you had guessed by now. My stepfather died when I was young and we needed money. So I went to the factory instead of school."

She was quiet, as if she didn't quite know what to say to that. Then, "That's not something I would judge you for. It wasn't your fault."

She hadn't known. And she didn't think less of him for it. "If it isn't that, then why? What's wrong with me?"

"Nothing." He could hear the exasperation in her voice and imagined her hands thrown up in the air. "Did you ever think that *I* might be unsuitable for *you*?"

Fifteen

"LET ME HELP."

Evangeline was folding the tent, much more neatly than she had been able to on the first few days of travel, and looked up to find Leo, arms outstretched.

"I'll stow it for you."

She opened her mouth to argue with him. This was the last task, other than hitching up the oxen. The camp was in its morning chaos, and she knew that Hollis would blow his bugle soon, calling for them to move out.

"I can—"

Leo didn't wait for her to make the independent statement. He took the awkward weight of canvas out of her hands and turned to stow it in the back of the wagon.

Evangeline looked around to complain to someone about his high-handedness, but only Sara was there at her feet, oblivious as she leaned down to peer at a grasshopper.

"C'mon," Leo said after he'd closed and latched the tailgate. "We've gotta get a move on."

Now she raised her eyebrows. "Come with you where? Sara and I usually stick close to the wagon."

"Not today. Today you're learning to ride."

She was sure she must've squawked or made some other noise of disagreement. Leo grinned.

"I can't. I've got Sara to look after."

"I've got everything worked out." Now there was a hint of impatience in his voice. "Alice can keep Sara occupied for one day. You said you wanted to be able to ride. Did you change your mind?"

"No." But it was frightening to even think about. She'd admitted it in more of an abstract way. One day, she'd learn to ride. One day, she'd be ready to live in the West.

Not *this* day. She wasn't ready.

"What about the wagon?" she asked almost desperately. "Who'll drive? And Father..."

"Coop will drive. And he'll keep an eye on your father."

Father had managed to walk for about a mile yesterday morning and another mile after lunch. He'd been pale and slow and had to stop twice when his cough grew so great that he couldn't stand upright. But he was fighting to return to health.

"Are you sure—" She didn't know whether she meant to protest that her father needed her or that Coop couldn't be trusted, not fully, but Leo took off his hat and swept one hand through his rumpled hair. It'd grown long over the past weeks on the trail. He needed a trim.

"Do you want to learn or not?" His eyes were bright, and she realized he'd caught her staring at his hand and hair.

She blushed.

It was as if what she'd admitted last night was there between them, as real and solid as a person. She'd all but admitted she fancied him.

"It won't be all fun and games," he said. "We'll be working with Collin to move the cattle."

His gaze held a clear challenge. And a belief that she could do it.

And there was Alice, hurrying around the family wagon. "Hello, Sara. Are we going to spend the day together?" She held out her hand, ignoring the tension in the air between the two adults.

Sara moved easily to join Alice, already talking about a grasshopper and a ladybug.

"Let's go then," Evangeline whispered.

She didn't miss the triumphant spark in Leo's eyes.

"But if I fall—" She didn't know what she intended to threaten him with.

He only fell into step beside her. "I won't let you fall."

I won't let you fall. Leo's words echoed in her thoughts a few moments later when she was face to face with the giant animal—taller than she was—and froze.

This was a bad idea.

The horse was huge. It could easily knock her down. Or throw her. Look at those hooves. Bigger than her own feet.

How did Leo intend to keep her from falling once she was sitting on the horse's back?

"He can sense your fear," Leo said.

"That poses a problem." She could barely exhale the words.

Collin was already saddled up and riding out past the cows scattered across a dozen yards outside the camp.

Leo didn't laugh at her or tell her that being afraid was silly.

He stepped behind her. Directly behind her, so that she felt his warmth at her back. He held a contraption that was a mess of leather straps in his left hand. He settled his right hand at her waist and she jumped.

He ignored her reaction and nudged her to step closer to the horse.

He must've intended to show her how to put the bridle on, but she could only grip his wrist as he slipped the bit between the horse's teeth. Her other arm hung uselessly at her side as he settled the leather strap over the horse's forehead and ears.

She gathered the courage to touch the horse's nose as Leo

buckled the bridle. The horse made a low noise and bobbed his head.

"He likes you," Leo said. "That's a start."

Was it?

Leo checked over the saddle Collin had already put on the animal and then stepped back to boost her into the saddle. She balked.

"Leo, I can't—"

The wagons were already rolling out, a cloud of dust rising.

And yet he showed no shred of impatience with her, only watched with eyes that showed his belief in her. "You won't be on your own. We'll ride double today, until you get a feel for him."

All day in the saddle, close to Leo? Riding double might be worse.

He held out his hand, palm up. He believed she could do this.

He was wrong, but he believed in her.

She placed her hand in his, and his strong fingers clasped hers. He didn't say anything else, and the jumbled emotions jangling inside her made her unable to hold his gaze.

She took a breath and moved next to the saddle.

"Step into my hand, then swing your opposite leg over."

"Astride?"

He only chuckled.

What did it matter? Impropriety was different out here. She'd seen women riding astride, some in trousers! Out here, everyone did what they had to in order to survive.

This wasn't any different.

He used his knee to brace while she gingerly put her foot into his palm. He lifted her easily, steadying her with a hand at her waist when she almost toppled over the horse's back and off the other side.

As Leo reached for the reins and slipped them over the

horse's head, she looked at the ground from her great height —even higher than sitting in the wagon seat.

And then Leo stepped into the stirrup. The leather gave a creak and the horse shifted a step as he swung up into the saddle behind her.

There wasn't a place she couldn't feel him behind her. She was enveloped in his warmth. His left arm was curved around her, holding the reins in front.

She felt as if she could jump out of her skin.

He didn't give her a chance to change her mind. What would she have done anyway if he'd let her down? Chase after the rolling wagons?

She felt the shift of his thighs, and then the horse was moving.

"See? It isn't so bad." His voice was a rumble at her back.

Yes, it was.

* * *

This hadn't been one of Leo's brightest ideas. He hadn't given enough thought to what it would be like to share the saddle with Evangeline all day.

Once she'd gotten over her initial bout of nerves, she'd engaged.

She asked him intelligent questions about the cattle. *How will you feed them through the winter? How will the herd multiply? Will you need to build a barn in Oregon?*

She heeded his lesson on using the reins and took over guiding the horse.

They were sitting so close that he physically felt the catch in her breath when she spotted a doe and fawn at the edge of a small copse of woods.

Every time she turned her head, tiny strands of her hair caught in the scruff on his chin.

She was driving him crazy. And it was his own fault.

Did you ever think that I might be unsuitable for you?

After what had passed between them last night, he'd gone to his bedroll with a keen sense of hope. She did want to be with him. She would've told him outright if she didn't. Yet she had some outlandish notion that something about her wasn't for him—and he wanted to tell her that she couldn't be more wrong.

She was as skittish as a newborn foal, so he needed to do this the right way. If he said or did the wrong thing, moved too fast, she'd send him away for good.

He couldn't pinpoint the exact moment things had changed for him. He only knew he wanted to be near her every moment of the day.

He had to tread carefully. He couldn't just blurt out how he felt about her. He knew that.

Collin was no help at all, keeping to the far side of the herd and constantly shooting knowing grins in Leo's direction.

Brothers.

When the wagon train stopped briefly at the noon hour, he and Collin slowed the cattle to a halt in a meadow next to a long gully that snaked through the ground. The meadow was flat enough to give them visibility if any of the cows started to wander off. They were far enough from the line of wagons that no one would walk out here on foot, not unless it was an emergency.

Leo pointed to a great old sycamore growing at the edge of the meadow.

Collin nodded and waved them on, so Leo told Evangeline to guide the horse over there.

The sycamore spread a canopy of leaves that provided shade for the horses. They'd need to find a creek and water the animals soon.

As they reined in, some kind of bird warbled above their heads.

Evangeline tipped her head back, probably to look for it. The sudden motion meant the back of her head bumped

Leo's shoulder. She froze. From this angle, sitting so close... If she turned her head a fraction, they would be face to face. Close enough to kiss.

Leo felt his heartbeat pulsing in the tips of his ears, the top of his head.

She quickly tipped her head down, now tense in the saddle. Holding herself away from him as much as she could.

And all of a sudden, Leo couldn't stand it anymore. A thick branch hung low enough over their heads that he could reach up and grab it.

"Steady with the reins," he said. He raised both arms, grabbed hold of that branch, and pulled himself out of the saddle, right up onto the tree. The branch didn't even wobble. The tree was big enough it might've been here for hundreds of years.

Evangeline gaped up at him, clearly surprised. "What are you doing?"

Collin gave a hearty laugh as he joined them beneath the shade of the tree. "I should've known you wouldn't be able to resist."

Evangeline glanced at Collin for clarification as Leo carefully edged toward the tree's trunk. He set one hand against it and stood up, using a new branch, at shoulder-height, to steady himself.

"Alice loaded my saddlebag with ham and biscuits. Start without me," Leo instructed.

"What are you doing?" Evangeline asked again.

She sounded so perplexed that he couldn't help the smile that twitched at his lips.

Meanwhile, Collin sidled up to Leo's horse and was already rifling through the saddlebag. He found the cloth-wrapped food that Alice had provided for them.

"Leo." Evangeline's tone held a note of concern as he climbed another branch. He must be a good fifteen feet off the ground now.

"I'm just having a little fun." Leo climbed two more

branches, the bark rough against his palms, the height making his stomach dip and reminding him he wasn't a kid anymore —he was old enough now to know how bad it would hurt if he fell.

He sat on a thick branch and let his feet dangle. "Quite a view from up here."

He could count the cattle if he had a mind to. Far off, where the wagons stood, he could see bodies moving around. Someone was bending to check a front wheel. Two kids huddled together, looking at something on the ground.

"Leo has always been the most adventurous one of us." Collin spoke the words through a mouth full of food.

Still on the horse's back, Evangeline had a biscuit in her hand. "I'm not sure I believe that."

Collin chewed and swallowed. "Believe it. Sometimes our mother would read us stories in the evening. Leo was the one who jumped up on the kitchen chair with a stick that he imagined into a sword so he could defend us from the pirates she was reading about."

Keeping his eyes on the horizon was easier than holding Evangeline's curious stare.

He remembered Mama reading, just like Collin said. It was a long time ago. Before his stepfather had died.

After Pa had died, Mama had taken on more hours at the factory. She'd come home so weary she could barely stay awake long enough to eat the supper he and Alice prepared. There'd been no more stories. No more joy.

Leo fought off the hopelessness that those memories brought back.

"Then you do like books." Evangeline said.

Leo realized Collin had shifted a few feet away, giving them a bit of privacy.

"Sure. I just can't read them." And it was still a sore subject for him.

There was a thoughtful pause before she spoke again.

"You must be happy on an adventure like this one. Seeing new land. Making a new life."

He went up another branch to keep from having to answer her.

He heard Collin mutter, "He didn't have a choice."

He didn't want to talk about that. Or think about it, either. "You ever climb a tree, Evie?"

He looked down to see her gaping at him. "What do you think?"

He grinned. "I think you've read about it, and that you want to try it."

The fact that she didn't immediately refuse was a sure sign.

"I'll come and get you." He clambered down until he was perched on the branch just above her head.

She wasn't quite tall enough in the saddle to reach it, and she probably didn't have enough strength in her arms to pull herself up onto it the way Leo had.

He sat down so his feet hung over the back of the horse's saddle.

"Better hand me my lunch," Leo said. "Collin gets hungry enough and he'll forget that I haven't eaten yet."

Collin rolled his eyes.

Evangeline rustled around in the saddlebag and handed Leo a cloth-wrapped bundle.

He tucked it into his breast pocket and reached one hand toward her, steadying himself against the tree with the other. "Ready?"

She shook her head no even as she reached up for him. One smooth tug and she sat on the branch next to him. Her knuckles were white as she clutched the tree.

"C'mon," Leo said.

They climbed several branches, back to where Leo had been before he'd invited her up there. When she needed it, Leo offered a hand up or a steadying touch to her waist.

Every touch made awareness crackle up and down his spine. Did she feel it too?

Finally, they stopped.

She stood closest to the trunk, one arm wrapped around it.

He braced his hand above her head. "Look." He used his free hand to gesture to the vista unfolded before them. Land stretched as far as the eye could see, mostly flat pasture but some trees here and there. There'd be craggy mountains sometime in the future. He couldn't wait to see them towering above.

"It's amazing, isn't it?" he asked. "And you never would've seen it if you'd kept your feet on the ground."

She didn't answer, and when he looked at her, her face was white as chalk.

"Evie, you with me?" He changed his hold on the tree to put his arm around her waist, his hand braced against the trunk. He edged closer and could feel her whole body trembling.

"I must be afraid of heights," she whispered. "I didn't know it until now."

"I won't let you fall." It was an echo of what he'd said earlier, a promise spoken to reassure her.

Somehow, they'd started out not even friends, and now his feelings for her had grown large and unwieldy.

He found himself gazing down into her face instead of looking at the landscape around them. She noticed too, turning her face but not before he saw the rosy blush climbing into her cheeks.

"What other adventures will you have?" she asked. "Two thousand dollars will take you a long way."

The reminder of the money made his stomach shift uneasily. "I'll use it to settle my family. Then when they're safe and taken care of, I can make my own way."

He focused on the far horizon, on the dreams that seemed a bit closer than they'd been before. "Maybe I'll go on a ship."

"You still want to be a pirate?"

He grinned at her. "Why not? You could come along. Be my first mate."

He'd only been teasing, but the warmth that had been in her eyes shifted to something cool.

"I barely made that river crossing, remember?" She edged back slightly, putting what distance between them that she could. "Can we go down now?"

Sixteen

"LEO, we need you. There's a situation."

The morning after climbing that tree, Leo sighed and looked longingly at his half-eaten plate of scrambled eggs and gravy. His stomach complained when he stood from near the fire, but there was nothing for it.

He'd agreed to be captain. And he was needed.

He followed Clarence Turnbull across the ring of wagons as everyone was waking up. And packing up.

At the Black family's wagon, two young men sat on the ground. He recognized them. Tony and Philip were sixteen and seventeen. Cousins. Old enough to know better. This wasn't the first time they'd been caught doing something they oughtn't.

Orrin Black stood over them, his hand on the butt of his gun, clearly angry. Tony's father, Eric, was striding across camp, his expression furious. Clarence stepped up next to Orrin, asking him in a low voice to lower his weapon.

All Leo felt was tired. He didn't want to do this today. He wanted to be out in the open air with Evangeline by his side.

And there was a part of him that was thankful that Coop was safe in his bedroll back at their wagon.

As soon as he thought it, he caught movement from the corner of his eye. He turned his head to see his brother sneaking away from a derelict wagon, one hand in his hair and his arm blocking his face. As if Leo wouldn't recognize his shirt or that shock of hair or the posture of the man he'd given up everything for.

Leo's anger burned.

Had Coop snuck out? Had he been out all night? Leo knew that wagon, knew Si Taylor and Frank Adams by sight. The two men had been involved in one of the earlier scuffles on this journey. They'd received a stern warning from Leo and Turnbull and hadn't been in trouble since. Leo had also seen them drinking from a flask by their campfire several nights, but what they did in camp wasn't his business. Unless they were making trouble.

Or involving his brother.

Orrin didn't wait for Leo to ask before making his accusation. "These two stole ten dollars right outta my wagon. My wife had put some aside for the trip into the fort tomorrow. This morning, it's gone."

Tony's father listened, his countenance grim. "What makes you think my son was involved?"

Orrin bristled. Clarence shifted his feet, edging slightly between the two men.

Leo frowned, playing the words back. Philip wasn't only Tony's cousin, he was traveling with the family. Why wasn't Eric defending him as well? That seemed off.

"They've been skulking around for days," Orrin said. "Last night, I caught Tony sneaking away from my wagon while Philip played lookout. I got on to 'em, but I didn't realize my wife had put the cash in easy reach. I didn't know it was gone until this morning."

That sounded pretty cut and dried.

"That still don't prove anything," Eric argued.

Leo wished the man wasn't involved. He was loud, and

other folks from neighboring wagons were looking on now. Owen was striding toward them, looking grim.

The quicker they got this resolved, the better.

"Empty your pockets," Leo said evenly to the two boys.

They both complied, turning their pants pockets inside out. There was nothing there.

If the theft had happened last night, there was no telling where the teens could've stashed the money.

"Take off your hats," Leo ordered.

The hats came off, were waved around.

"We didn't do nothin'," Philip said. But his words were almost a snigger, and he shot a glance at his cousin that was on the edge of being smug.

Owen had stopped and conferred with Clarence in a low voice, and now he strode over to Leo. He leaned close. "You can't do anything if there's no evidence they took the money. Maybe his wife put it somewhere else. Maybe it's not even missing."

While Owen spoke, Philip shot a sly grin at his cousin. He was involved somehow. Leo's gut told him so.

Orrin had gone past simply being angry. "My wife and I need that money. We've got to buy flour and corn."

Leo didn't like the desperation in the man's voice. He needed to ask Alice to check on Orrin's wife later. Find out what they and the other travelers could do to help.

"My son didn't take your money," Eric said. He turned to his son. "C'mon."

The kid took one limping step and Leo called out, "Hold on."

He had a little niggle of a memory of Alice finding smokes inside one of Coop's boots when he'd been fourteen. They'd had a huge row over it at the time.

"Pull off your boots," Leo said to the boys.

"No," came Tony's instant refusal.

Owen seemed to grow larger at Leo's side. "Take them off, or we'll do it for you."

Eric was silent, anger tightening his eyes.

Reluctantly, both teens sat down and pulled off their left boot.

When they pulled off their right, dollar bills fluttered to the ground from both boys' boots.

Leo felt no satisfaction as Orrin rushed forward and knelt on the ground to retrieve his missing money.

Tony stood with his head down, shame written on the set of his shoulders while his father berated him. Philip stared around with his chin jutted, clearly unrepentant.

Leo conferred with Clarence and Owen.

"We gotta kick them out," Clarence said.

"Hollis said there'd be no mercy for anybody caught stealing," Owen said.

Leo couldn't stand the thought of it. Eric was pale, staring at them as they spoke in their circle. He had a wife and two daughters, both younger than Tony. This was going to affect them, too.

Leo couldn't stop thinking about the way Evangeline had held a drowsing Sara at the fire last night. Compassion stirred for the man in this position.

"Hollis set the rules before we left Independence," Owen said. "It's our job to enforce them." He didn't sound any happier about it than Leo felt.

But Owen was right. Although it was the last thing he wanted to do, Leo strode over to Eric and said, "Your son and nephew committed a crime. They can't stay on the wagon train. You can leave them at the fort, or your family can choose to stay with them, but the two of them aren't welcome any longer."

"And you'd better keep them out of trouble until we reach the fort," Orrin called out.

Eric was white-faced but didn't protest. That didn't mean he wouldn't seek Leo out later and beg for leniency.

But Leo wouldn't relent. He'd make sure Hollis knew what was going on.

He knew why Hollis had set the rules. If there was no order, no consequences on the wagon train, chaos would ensue. People could get hurt, or even killed, over the least provocation. It was stressful enough to travel so far through dangerous terrain without knowing what awaited them. It was a reminder of the weight on his own shoulders. What had Coop been up to last night or this morning?

Leo was kidding himself if he thought his brother was a changed man. But what was he going to do about it?

He trudged back to his own campsite, appetite gone.

He caught sight of Evangeline packing something away in the wagon. The breeze was blowing strands of her hair against her cheek and her skirts billowed out behind her. He'd intended for everything to go back to normal today, to drive her wagon again.

But he just couldn't stand it. Not after what'd happened.

Coop was nowhere in sight, and he couldn't forget that he still needed to confront his brother.

"We're riding again today," he told her.

"I can't saddle Alice with Sara again."

Why couldn't she just be easy?

Because she was Evangeline. And he liked her the way she was.

"Fine. We'll take Sara with us."

* * *

Evangeline knew Leo had had a tough morning. She tried not to listen to camp gossip but it seemed to find her anyway.

His movements as he saddled the bay horse they had ridden yesterday were coiled with leashed tension.

"Are you sure this is a good idea?" she asked. She had Sara by the hand, and the girl was staring avidly at the horse.

Evangeline couldn't fathom how he meant to bring the toddler along. Did he intend for all three of them to ride on the horse?

"It's a fine idea."

When Coop walked over to them, biscuits still in hand from breakfast, Leo tensed.

"Do you mind watching over my father again today?" she asked Coop. She wanted to take Leo's tension away, silly as that intention seemed.

"I don't mind," Coop said easily. "Your dad is real knowledgeable about business. I probably pestered him too much yesterday, but he let me ask a bunch of questions."

"Father loves to talk business."

If there was one thing she could be assured of, it was that.

"He was telling me some of the plans he has for the new mill in the Willamette valley. Maybe I'll end up working there."

She smiled at Coop, but Leo now gripped the edges of the saddle, his knuckles white. He looked over and skewered Coop with his stare. "I need to talk to you when we make camp."

Coop bristled. Evangeline would have, too, given Leo's bossy voice.

"Why don't you just talk to me now?" Coop's words were calm, but his posture was edgy. Ready for a fight.

"Tonight," Leo said.

"You ready?" Leo turned to her, as if his brother wasn't even standing there. Whatever was going on between them, he didn't want her to witness it.

She didn't know whether she really was, but she nodded and allowed him to boost her up into the seat. She was surprised that he reached for the stirrups and started adjusting them to fit her feet. Even more surprised when he moved away from the bay and over to Collin's gray and silver flecked horse and began to saddle up.

"You're not riding with me?" She couldn't help the way her voice squeaked a bit.

He shook his head, his hands moving quickly over the saddle.

"I can't ride by myself."

There was something almost fierce in his smile. "You're ready. You've come a long way since Independence. You can drive that wagon on your own. Cook supper and everything. You just need to trust in yourself."

He hefted Sara into his arms and stepped up easily into the saddle, settling the girl in his lap.

Sara clapped her hands, delighted with this adventure.

Leo wheeled his horse and was clearly waiting for her. "Collin will be wanting his breakfast. Let's go relieve him."

Her heart thrummed hard in her chest as she felt the power of the animal beneath her. She'd ridden with Leo yesterday, but this was different. What if she got thrown off?

She had the reins between her fingers. She was in charge.

You need to trust in yourself. She hadn't done that for a very long time.

Leo thought she could do this. He and Sara were watching. There was really no question. She wasn't going to let fear win.

She nudged the horse with her legs, the way she remembered Leo doing yesterday, and felt momentary terror and elation as the animal began to walk.

Leo grinned at her, but she didn't miss the way his eyes tracked back to camp before he led the way out to where the cattle had passed the night.

As the morning passed, Sara was clearly having an outrageous amount of fun.

Who knew pushing cows could be anything but work? When they rode further apart than shouting distance, Leo gestured with his arms to direct Evangeline. Leo didn't complain when part of the herd got a little too far away and he had to chase them back down.

As they lunched on hard tack, he told Sara silly stories about a baby cow that had her laughing.

Evangeline was holding her own.

She hadn't expected days like this on their journey. She'd

planned a life for Sara and a way to make it happen by encouraging Father to start a new business out in the West. When she'd imagined the future, she was the one who'd disappeared. Everything was for Sara's happiness, Father's satisfaction.

But today she wondered whether she couldn't take small snatches of happiness as they came. She didn't need much.

As the afternoon sun was waning, Evangeline found herself watching Leo more than the cattle. Sara had finally succumbed to exhaustion, her head tipped against him as she slept. Leo held her easily, supporting her weight as he edged his horse around a cow that really wanted to go up the hill.

He would be a good father.

Evangeline stopped short on the heels of that thought. Her horse noticed the sudden tension, so she forced herself to relax her body.

It didn't matter whether or not Leo would be a good father.

Once this journey was over, he would be out of her life, and Sara's too.

From what he'd told her and what she'd put together by talking with Alice, he had been raising Coop and Collin and taking care of Alice since he was a boy.

He'd told her he wanted adventure. Not to be saddled with another small child to take care of.

Evangeline would never abandon Sara. Never.

Which meant that no matter what softer feelings she had for him, they didn't matter.

She realized with a sense of impending doom that she had let Leo in. She hadn't meant to. His friendship meant a lot to her, and she didn't want things to change between them. But she liked him. He was strong and courageous. Yet gentle and patient with Sara.

From a distance, they could see the wagons circling. Leo hailed her with a raised hand. She rode to meet him behind the group of cattle.

"We're missing one," he said.

Oh no. It was probably her fault.

"There were a couple that seem determined to get into that wild bramble."

She remembered the place he was talking about. Wild plum trees with spiky branches had grown up over the lip of a small washed-out gully.

"I can ride back and see if I can find it," she said.

"We'll both go."

She tried not to show her relief, but somehow, he knew. The sun was setting and there was still time before it got dark, but she didn't want to be out here alone once night fell.

They left the herd behind, the animals slow and sleepy after a long day of moving.

It gave them a chance to ride closer. Sure enough, when they reached the plum thicket and gully, the cow was there at the bottom. Leo pointed out a small game trail, and Evangeline turned her horse to descend it.

"Easy, there," he cautioned.

Something rustled in the brush at the horse's feet. Evangeline flinched.

The horse tensed as if to bolt and time seemed to slow down. Leo grabbed her horse's reins just beneath its bridle as a rabbit burst out of the brush and flew underneath the horse's feet.

Evangeline's heart battered against her sternum like a bird's wings, fast and fluttery. Leo settled the horse with a word.

And somehow, Sara still slept against him.

Leo sidled his horse closer and touched her elbow. "You okay?"

She wasn't okay. He must've seen it in her wide eyes because he ducked his head and kissed her.

His lips were warm and gentle, his affection as steady and sure as the man himself. She wanted to reach her arms around his neck, hold him closer.

She couldn't do this.

She turned her face away, breaking the kiss.

What had she done?

Seventeen

"HE IS GOOD WITH HER."

Evangeline startled. She was supposed to be watching the sizzling venison in the pan over the fire, but she flushed guiltily when father's words registered and she realized she was staring at Leo and Sara playing a mixed up game of tag in the field just outside the ring of wagons.

The sun was already up, but Hollis had declared today would be a short day, so no one was rushing to have breakfast or get packed.

Evangeline had offered to make breakfast. Alice deserved to rest, too, though Evangeline suspected she was staying in her tent to avoid Rob Braddock. The man had skulked around the campsite last night until Alice's brothers had come into camp.

"What, Father?" She pretended she hadn't heard him, turning an innocent expression his direction.

Father had more color in his cheeks. His cough still surprised him at times, and sometimes doubled him over, but he was slowly improving.

Just looking at him made tears spring to Evangeline's eyes.

Apparently, Father wasn't to be deterred. He nodded toward Leo and Sara. "Your young man is good with her."

"He's not my young man." The words were automatic, an instant denial. And then she thought of the way his lips had brushed hers last night, and her face burned.

Perhaps Father wouldn't notice.

But his stare was too intent. "Why not?" he asked in his frank way.

She turned the potatoes in the skillet, needing to give her hands a job, needing not to look at him.

"You know why." Saying the words aloud made the place behind her nose sting. Echoes of unkind voices from the past played in her mind.

She sniffed once and pushed away those memories. "Leo and I made a deal." She could pretend that's what she meant.

"So change the deal." He made it sound so simple, ever the businessman. Used to getting what he wanted.

"I can't," she hissed, turning her head so that the words were directed at him and not the pan. "You know I can't."

"Of course you can change your mind. Your mother did it all the time."

Alice emerged from her tent, yawning and stretching. Evangeline became conscious of how Father's voice might carry. She turned her back to the cookfire so she could face father on his stool.

She lowered her voice. "Leo wants freedom and adventure. He told me so himself. And being with *me*," she meant her and Sara, "would be the opposite of that."

She thought of it all the time. She couldn't help it. She replayed those moments standing close together in the top of a tree over and over in her mind. *Maybe I'll go on a ship.*

And he'd kissed her yesterday. Because he thought she was unencumbered and free herself. He didn't know that Sara was hers, that she'd dedicated her life to her little girl.

Father was watching her, and she didn't like the thunderous expression growing on his face. "I thought we came West for a new beginning."

"For Sara." Tears pricked her eyes in earnest.

"For Sara, and for you." His words were clipped and intense.

"No. Sara will grow up and never know my shame. She'll marry someone who loves her deeply. She'll be happy."

It was all Evangeline wanted. Her daughter's happiness.

But Father wore a stubborn expression. "I didn't sell my company and everything we owned—we didn't come all this way so that you could grow old alone. Every time you pushed for this, for a new start, I thought you meant for both of you."

"No." Even her words sounded soggy now. She brushed wetness from her cheek with one hand. "For Sara. Only for Sara."

"That's ridiculous. That young man cares about you. Anyone with eyes can see it. You're leading him on." His sharp words were like a slap. She knew what he thought of her. She'd endured his cold silence when she'd told him she was pregnant, had weathered months of him barely speaking to her.

She'd imagined their thoughts were aligned. That he understood why Sara couldn't grow up in their Boston neighborhood.

The way he looked at her now said otherwise.

"Everything all right?" Leo strode into their little bubble, breaking it. Suddenly, Evangeline could hear a squabble between two young children, a bird chirping, the venison sizzling.

She turned and bent over the pan on the fire quickly, afraid of what Leo might see on her face. She surreptitiously used her apron to dry her face.

She could hear Sara talking to Alice nearby.

There was no privacy to be had in this camp. Had anyone overheard their conversation? She wracked her brain, trying to remember whether she'd said anything about Sara, about her parentage.

She was off-kilter and at first didn't register Leo striding to her. He cupped one of her elbows in his big, warm hand, raised her upright so she was forced to look him in the eye.

"Hey. Is everything all right?"

She felt all of it choking her. Right there, close enough behind her throat that it could pour out so easily. As tenuous and fragile as a soap bubble. So easy to burst.

She couldn't let it.

Sara's future happiness depended on her.

"Of course everything is all right." She formed a smile and could only hope he believed her. She couldn't quite look him in the eye so her gaze skipped over his shoulder.

He leaned in closer and brushed a kiss on her cheek. "I've gotta check with Owen about those boys who were causing trouble. Save me some breakfast?"

She made some response that must've satisfied him, because he left. Alice joined her with Sara, and Evangeline began dishing out the venison and potatoes.

The confrontation with her father left her feeling raw. Not because of the wanting. That was always with her. That was the worst of it. She wanted Leo's kindness, his steady presence, even his kisses.

But she couldn't have any of it. She'd made a vow that Sara wouldn't know hardship or shame because of her.

Yet Father's blunt words had made one thing clear: Evangeline couldn't go on like this. She was going to hurt Leo.

And she couldn't stand that, either.

* * *

"How do you court someone like Evangeline?" Leo felt himself flush even as he asked the question. Alice's brows raised in amusement. He couldn't even find it in himself to care.

"I thought you were already courting her," Alice said.

"It's complicated. She is..."

"She's lovely, even though I thought she was snobbish in the beginning."

So had he, but he didn't say that. He still didn't know why she kept walls between them. But he wanted to find out.

"She's used to the finer things in life," he admitted. "I can't give her that."

Alice's gaze went far off. "Money isn't everything. Some people have all the money in the world and are still clueless to the needs of those around them."

What was she... was she talking about Braddock now?

He was toting the big metal tub that Alice used when she wanted a good washing. Tonight, after supper, she asked him to fill it up for her. He usually would've done it all on his own, but he'd made noises about needing someone to help lug it back to camp and managed to pull her away for this private conversation.

"You should just be yourself," Alice said.

To which he snorted skeptically.

"I'm not joshing. You are an excellent provider. You have a kind heart, and you are a good leader."

He couldn't dispute that. The men he had worked with in the powder mill had always looked to him for advice, even when it was something outside of the mill work.

"And you're smart," Alice finished with a firm nod.

"No, I'm not."

Alice looked affronted by his instant denial.

When they reached the creek, he bent to submerge the tub into the water to fill it.

"So what if you don't have a lot of book learning?" Alice preached like the loyal sister she was. "You can't learn every-thing in life from books."

That made him smile, because it made him think of Evan-geline, the woman who had memorized so many facts because she was nervous about coming on this journey.

"Someone as intelligent as Evangeline probably wants to be with somebody who has a lot of book smarts."

Alice looked at him with her brows drawn. "I thought you were already together."

Stumbling over his words, he ended up explaining the deal to her. She sat on the bank of the river, elbows on her knees, scowling at him. "I can't believe you. I'm terribly disappointed."

"I'm sorry for lying to you." He wouldn't blame it on Evangeline. He'd gone along with her plan.

"Not about that," she said. "All this time, I thought Evangeline was going to be my sister-in-law."

For a moment, he felt as if he had been punched in the chest. All of the air was suddenly gone from his lungs.

He hadn't let himself think of what marriage to Evangeline might be like. He knew he wanted to be with her, but that seemed out of the realm of possibility.

"That's why I need your help. I deeply admire her, and I want to convince her that she should give me a chance for real."

Alice's brows drew together. "You admire her?" Her words dripped with disbelief. "I think you meant to say you've fallen for her."

There was no way he was admitting that to his sister. Not when he couldn't even admit it to himself. Evangeline was special. And he wanted her in his life. That was enough for now.

"Books are definitely the way to her heart," Alice said.

He wanted to protest, wanted to shout his frustration that he couldn't learn to read at this late stage.

Alice seemed to understand his conundrum. She shook her head. "I don't think it will bother her that you don't know how to read."

"She already knows."

Alice nodded. "Good. She likes you. I'm sure of it."

Leo's stomach jumped. Could Alice be right? He didn't dare hope.

"Evangeline loves to read," Alice said. "There are other folks in the wagon train who've brought books with them. Everyone's depleted their supplies. There will be more forts, but they'll need a way to buy the flour or sugar they need. What if you bought some books for Evangeline, as gifts?"

He shook his head. "I'm not using our family's money to buy courting gifts." Who knew what they would face when they got to the Willamette Valley? He needed to save their resources. "But maybe I could do some trading. Maybe hunt for someone or help repair a wagon."

"Or something else," Alice added excitedly.

He liked this idea, and it was clear that she did too.

"You can give her the gifts," Alice said. "But you've got to make it clear that your intention is to court her for real."

He sort of thought he had already been doing that with kisses. But when he told Alice that she seemed appalled.

"You can't just go around kissing her. You've got to prove that you are serious about her first."

Was Alice kidding?

She raised her brows, clearly waiting for a response.

"Fine. No more kissing. For now," he added.

Alice studied him intently, making no move to stand up from the creek bank. "We should probably give you a haircut. And you should definitely think about shaving the scruff off your face more often."

She wanted him to what?

Eighteen

WHEN EVANGELINE OPENED the tent flap on the second morning, she almost stepped on it.

It was only because she reacted quickly and caught her balance that she didn't.

She bent and picked up the mystery item.

It was a book. A book with a single wildflower lying on top of it.

One of her hands curved around the spine while the other picked up the flower. It was shaped like a daisy, with a brown center, but the petals were painted red and yellow.

She glanced around her, but no one in the closest wagons were stirring yet.

Her heart raced as she clutched the flower in one hand and opened the cover. The hard cloth rubbed against her hand, and she felt the sense of anticipation that always came when she opened a new book. What would she find inside?

It was a novel. About a pirate.

She bit her lip, glancing up and all around, trying to hide the sunny smile that wanted to escape. Leo. It had to be from Leo.

A grumble from Sara, behind her in the tent and waiting to leave, set her feet to moving.

She'd walked several steps, only one ear on Sara's chatter about the tiny clouds dotting the sky, before she realized she was hugging the book to her chest.

She should've left it at the tent. She should put it down right now, leave it in the grass and walk away, though the thought made her shudder.

She should not keep the book snug against her body. Just like she should not keep Leo close to her heart.

But she couldn't quite let go of the book as she and Sara walked in the dappled shade of a grove of scrub oaks.

That young man cares about you. Anyone with eyes can see it. You're leading him on. She had tossed and turned all night, remembering her father's words.

Father wanted her to fall in love.

To marry.

How could she, when falling in love had cost her so dearly?

And Leo still didn't know about Sara's parentage.

She tried to imagine telling him, but he was so steadfastly moral. So upright.

How could he understand the grave mistake she'd made? How could he forgive her when she couldn't forgive herself?

It was better if she didn't consider it. Besides, Leo could've meant a lot of things by leaving the book for her. Maybe he wanted her to teach him how to read. Maybe he wanted her to read it to Sara.

It didn't have to mean anything romantic.

It was only when she and Sara were making their way back to camp after a few private moments in the woods that she came across Leo and realized her foolishness.

"Lee!" Sara shouted when they were still a piece off.

Leo turned from where he'd been securing one of Alice's pots to the outside of his wagon.

Sara set out at a run, and he turned away from his task to scoop her into his arms.

"Hullo, Sara-girl. Didja find any interesting bugs this morning?"

Evangeline pulled a face, and he chuckled for a moment, even as he listened raptly to Sara's chatter about a leaf she'd seen floating down the creek.

Last night, Sara had found a critter roughly the length of Evangeline's hand with what seemed to be hundreds of legs. It had crawled along the ground in such a creepy way that she'd felt as if tiny little insect feet were crawling on her all evening long. Leo had caught her eye across the fire at supper and grinned when he'd noticed her shiver.

She was glad one of them could laugh about it.

His gaze drifted to her as Sara's story got longer and longer. He took in the book Evangeline still clutched to her chest and his gaze grew warmer.

That was the moment she knew she'd let herself get in too deep with Leo Mason. When he looked at her with that affectionate warmth, she felt... something.

She didn't dare give it a name.

She'd ignored it for too long. Maybe she'd thought if she suppressed it, it would go away. She'd allowed herself to fall for Jeremy so effortlessly that she should've been able to prevent it from happening again, if she just tried hard enough.

But she had never expected Leo. Leo, who put his family first, even beyond his own needs. Who treated Sara like a valued niece. Who had found and gifted this book to Evangeline simply because he could.

She was falling for him.

Her chest felt tight and her skin prickled all over, as if it had somehow grown too tight for her body. She dropped the book away from her chest and stared at its cover through eyes that couldn't seem to focus.

He must've seen the panic registering on her face, because he took a step closer to her, interrupting Sara mid-sentence.

"What's the matter? You don't like it?"

It wasn't that. And with the noise of camp waking up, neighbors much too close and activity all around, she couldn't find words.

She needed to tell him that she couldn't do this.

But what emerged was, "Do you think I could ride the herd again today?"

She smoothed her expression and looked up to see his response.

His brows were creased. "I already sent Coop out. It's probably too late to ask him to drive the wagon."

"That's all right. I'll ride with Coop. I can do it. And I'll ask Alice to take Sara for the day."

She'd put it in a way she knew he couldn't easily refuse.

He wanted to say something, maybe to ask her what was going on, but someone hailed him from a dozen yards away.

"Come along, Sara." She scooped Sara out of his arms and rushed away before he could protest.

Her face burned as she hurried to Alice.

She was a coward. She knew she should give back the book. Tell Leo she didn't want it, didn't want him.

Lie through her teeth.

She'd already woven such a web of lies. He wouldn't want her if he knew the truth.

She couldn't bear thinking about it—about any of it. A day alone, focusing on the cattle and the land, would help her clear her mind.

And then she'd have to figure out a way to break Leo's heart.

And her own.

* * *

"You're a good egg, young man."

"Thank you, ma'am." Collin didn't look up from the yoke as he finished fixing it in place over the Fairfaxs' second ox. His biceps quivered as he put the last pin in the bow.

"Hauling water last night and now this."

"My pleasure, ma'am."

Irene Fairfax was Steven's aunt, though Collin had only seen her outside of the wagon once. She seemed frail and sickly, a bulky shawl wrapped around her hunched shoulders and leaning on a walking stick.

Come to think of it, she didn't look that old. She had a few streaks of silver in her hair at her temples, but her skin was unwrinkled.

Another mystery about the Fairfax family.

It'd been two weeks since the hunting party, and Collin couldn't shake the sense that something was fishy about this family. He'd hesitated to bring it up to Leo, even though his brother was captain. He had enough to worry about.

Last night, after Hollis had called a halt, Collin had witnessed Steven get thrown from his massive horse. The young man had scrambled to his feet, but it was clear from the way he favored his left arm that something was wrong. Collin had followed him to his wagon, and when he'd asked whether he could help with anything, a panicked Maddie had asked for a bath. Or rather, for pails of water from the creek.

Collin thought he might've strained a muscle in his shoulder after hauling so many pails of water. By the time he had carried the second pail back to camp, Maddie and Steven had disappeared, their younger brother, Louis, the only one left in camp. The boy had sat on a barrel with his hat pulled low over his face, whittling on a small chunk of wood.

Collin had filled up their washtub with water and hung around another couple minutes, wanting to see if they needed anything else. It'd quickly gotten awkward with him and Louis sitting in silence, so he'd gone.

He was more determined than ever to discover what was

going on with the family. By now, his curiosity had grown insatiable.

This morning, he'd been up before dawn, and when he'd gone by the Fairfax's campsite and seen their oxen weren't hitched yet, he'd started the task himself.

"What're you doing?" Steven's strident voice brought Collin's head up. He gave the nearest ox one last pat on the rump.

Irene was nowhere to be seen, and the young man stood close, with one hand cocked on his hip, the other held gingerly by his side. Still sore?

"Helping out," Collin said evenly.

"Who asked you to do that?" Steven seemed furious that Collin had hitched up the team for him.

Collin bristled. "You could try saying 'thank you'."

"He offered to help." There was Irene, rounding the wagon again, a pail in her hand. He had a fervent hope she wasn't going to ask him to fetch more water.

"I'm perfectly capable of hitching up the wagon." But Steven's face was pale, and he seemed to be gritting his teeth.

"Nobody said you weren't capable," Collin said. "Don't get your trousers in a hitch. I saw you get thrown last night. How's your arm?"

"Fine," Steven bit out.

Irene passed close behind Steven and whispered something Collin couldn't hear. Whatever it was, it riled the boy up even more. Collin watched in fascination as he visibly pulled his temper back under control.

"Thanks for your help," Steven muttered.

He almost sounded sincere. Why had Collin bothered? He was already behind on getting his own horse saddled.

But his curiosity about the family remained. He wasn't going to let a little rudeness get in the way of his self-imposed mission.

"You have Maddie look at your arm? What'd she think?"

Steven opened his mouth to retort—Collin saw it coming

—but Irene interrupted from where she stood near the front wagon wheel. "Is that why you've been coming around lately? You sweet on Maddie?"

The unexpected words had both Collin and Steven gaping at Irene, even though it took a moment for the words to register, at least for Collin.

Steven's shock turned to scowling.

"Uhh—"

Whatever denial he was going to make was cut off by Steven's flashing eyes. "Maddie isn't interested in him."

It was Collin's turn to bristle. "How do you know?"

"I just know."

The young man had taken a step closer, so Collin did, too. Steven was more than a head shorter than him and with his pale face, it seemed like a stiff wind could knock him over.

But he didn't back down, and there was fire in his eyes. "My sister doesn't want you to come courting."

Collin had a protective older brother, but Steven's bossy tone rivaled what he'd heard from Leo. "I'll believe it when she tells me herself."

What was he doing? He wasn't interested in Maddie, not romantically. She was pretty enough, but he'd come into their campsite to try and figure out what secrets Steven and Irene were hiding.

Irene tottered toward the dying fire with the pail, obviously too heavy for her.

Collin rushed over, taking it from her hand.

Steven was two paces behind. "I'll do that."

But Collin had already poured the water on the few remaining embers. Smoke and steam obscured Steven from view as the fire hissed and spat.

And then a gust of wind blew the smoke away to reveal Steven's glare.

"Don't you need to get your own wagon on the road?" the kid snapped.

"In a minute."

Leo was probably having a conniption, not knowing where Collin was. He worried enough because Coop hadn't been pulling his weight—and Leo didn't even know the extent of it.

But Collin's feet seemed to be glued to the ground as he continued to stare at Steven. There was something about the kid that drew Collin. Maybe it was the fire in his eyes, a fire that resonated with Collin. Maybe it was his protectiveness.

Or maybe it was the fact that Collin couldn't stand not knowing his secret.

"Here's Maddie now." Irene's voice made Collin blink, and he broke the staring contest.

Maddie rushed into camp, clearly just come from washing up at the creek. Louis was right behind her.

Maddie's cheeks glowed pink from the scrubbing she must've given them. Her eyes were the same clear blue as Steven's. She looked a lot like her brother. The same elfin features...

He narrowed his eyes, realization stealing over him.

He turned to look at Steven again, but the young man had already turned away, busying himself with loading up the last few crates into the back of the wagon. One-handed.

Collin's nose twitched with the feeling he was getting closer to figuring this out. He went to pick up the last crate, but Steven rushed ahead and whipped it up into his arms. He turned his back before Collin could study his features.

And the bugle sounded, which meant Collin's time was up. Leo would surely be looking for him now.

But he also couldn't help himself. He turned back to where Irene and Maddie were whispering at a furious pace.

"Miss Maddie, would you like to go walking tonight after supper?"

Her eyes widened with a hint of the same panic he'd seen on her face last night. Her gaze darted to Steven. He caught motion from the corner of his eye, but when he glanced in the young man's direction, the kid was looking off in the distance.

He smiled charmingly at Maddie.

"I... I guess so."

From behind him, he heard Steven grunt.

Collin doffed his hat and grinned at Irene and Maddie before he strode away.

Nineteen

THAT AFTERNOON, Hollis called an early halt because of dark clouds building on the horizon. A storm was coming.

Leo built a fire for Alice, lugged her cookpot out of the wagon, and distracted Sara long enough for Alice to start supper. There was still no sign of Coop or Evangeline. Their absence made him antsy.

Where were they?

Evangeline had been acting strangely this morning. Why had she wanted to spend the day in the saddle without him? He wanted—needed—to make sure she was all right.

He'd taken Alice's advice about the book, but he was afraid he'd mucked it up somehow.

Those storm clouds were getting darker. Every once in a while, a flash of lightning lit up the darkening sky.

Collin had gone out to relieve Coop for the evening. Any minute now, Coop and Evangeline would ride over that hill and come into camp.

And he intended to tell Evangeline how he felt. He couldn't wait any longer.

But a few moments later, when rapid hoofbeats drummed against the ground, it was Collin who rode in.

Leo jumped to his feet. "What's wrong? Where's Evie? And Coop?"

Collin shook his head. "The cattle are all bunched up, like they should be. But one's missing. And there's no sign of Coop or Evie."

Leo's stomach plunged. "Can I have your horse?"

Collin was already swinging out of the saddle. "That's what I thought you'd say. I'll see if I can borrow a mount and follow."

If the pair was in trouble, Leo might need the help.

What could've happened to them? Anything was the answer. They'd passed a steep ravine two miles back, one with a rolling creek deep below. Before that, early this morning, there'd been a river crossing. The water had been flat and slow-moving, but what if something had gone wrong and Leo didn't even know about it?

Thunder rolled. His horse's ears twitched.

The air turned thick and peaty, and the clouds overhead grew more menacing by the second. Over an hour until sunset but the sky was growing dark already.

He hadn't thought to grab a lantern.

If Evangeline was out here, how would he see her?

He fumed internally, anger directed at his brother. Evangeline was a novice rider. Why had Coop let her go after a missing cow? What if she was injured?

Time passed and his worry grew. He approached the edge of the river without finding Coop or Evangeline. He glanced left and then right. Which way should he go? What if they hadn't even come this way? The vast western plains spread out all around him. His stomach knotted. What should he do?

He uttered every prayer he could think of. His horse's ears twitched again. A far off rumble of thunder sounded.

He couldn't just stay here.

He wheeled his horse to the right, instinct driving him.

He followed the riverbank, straining his eyes for any sign, any track.

He followed the river around a bend and there, a dozen yards away, was Coop, on his horse.

Leo shouted, and his brother turned his horse to meet him. He looked grim.

"There's a cow missing."

"I don't care about the cow," Leo said. "Where's Evangeline?"

Coop shook his head. Leo wanted to punch him "I don't know. I was... distracted when we rolled into camp."

Distracted? No. Coop had stumbled over that word. There was something he wasn't saying, but Leo would have to deal with that later.

"I started counting heads, and by the time I realized there was one missing, Evangeline hadn't shown up either. I think she must've gone after it."

On her own? This was worse than Leo had thought.

"She's not a strong rider. Not yet."

"You sent her out on that horse," Coop argued.

"I didn't send her anywhere!" Leo roared. She'd insisted on riding today. "I should've known you wouldn't be able to watch out for someone else, someone I care about."

Coop flinched as if Leo had struck him.

"We're wasting time," Leo said. He nudged his mount into a fast walk, knowing that every minute it was growing darker.

Where was Evangeline? Was she afraid? Was she injured?

Coop rode a few yards beside him. Not speaking, thank goodness. Leo didn't think he could stand hearing his brother's excuses right now.

It grew almost too dark to see, but Leo kept soldiering on.

Gradually, the riverbank separated from the water until it was more of a straight drop-off down to the water. The river had narrowed, which meant the water would be deeper, the current stronger. Leo could hear the danger in the rushing water.

Had they come too far?

Then Leo spotted something ahead. He rode a few more paces before reining in his horse.

The bank had given way. Soil had crumbled down into the water in a mini-avalanche.

If something—or someone—had been there when it'd happened, they would've been swept into the river.

Lightning flashed, and his eye caught movement across the rushing water. Past the bank, a riderless horse paced nervously, reins dragging the ground.

Leo's heart caught in his chest. Where was Evangeline?

"I'm going to backtrack and cross the river," Coop called.

"I don't care about the horse," Leo returned as the first spatters of rain landed on his hat brim. "We need to find Evie."

"If her horse is over there, she might be too."

Leo had no argument to counter that, and he knew it wouldn't change his stubborn brother's mind anyway.

Coop took off with a "hiyah!" while Leo kept moving downriver, straining his eyes for any sign of Evangeline. Had she been wearing her blue dress today? He thought so, but his memories of this morning were muddled with his terror of what might've happened to her. He couldn't think straight.

Lightning flashed again. Thunder rolled.

His horse balked, but Leo steadied it.

Coop galloped up to the river's edge on the opposite side. Up ahead, the river followed another bend where a small island sat out in the deep current, two scraggly trees growing out of it.

Coop shouted.

Leo couldn't make out the words, but his brother was waving. No, pointing.

Lightning flashed, illuminating a heap of fabric against the darkness of the bank of that island.

No.

That had to be Evangeline, lying facedown. She wasn't moving.

He looked for a way he might get off this high bank and down to the water. It was too steep, but he couldn't waste the time to go upriver and then swim downstream.

Evangeline needed help. And she needed it now.

"Don't!"

He heard Coop's shout on the wind but ignored it.

There was one spot where a deer path trailed down toward the water. It was narrow, and if the muddy bank crumbled beneath his horse's feet, he'd be thrown into the dangerous water.

He went anyway.

* * *

Evangeline pressed her face to the ground, trying to breathe. Her fingers made claws that sank into the muddy bank.

She was alive.

But the rain now pouring down, soaking her back and head even more, had darkened the sky. River water pulled at her legs and sodden clothes weighed her down.

She knew her situation was hopeless.

She just didn't want to believe it.

She'd been tracking the cow that had wandered off, but it hadn't wanted to be caught and stayed yards in front of her.

By the time she realized she should have stopped and gone back for Coop, she had lost all sense of direction and only knew she was far from camp.

So she'd kept following that ornery cow. Someone would come for it, right?

And then somehow the ground had fallen away beneath her horse's feet. She'd tumbled out of the saddle as they'd both plunged in the murky, fast-moving water.

She'd been swept away, choking on the water that filled

her mouth and nose, unable to keep her head above water in the powerful current. Her dress had tangled around her legs.

Through sheer luck, she'd given one mighty kick just as a rogue wave had pushed her forward, and she'd landed on this spit of land.

She hadn't known it was only a tiny sliver of sand and two scraggly trees. She'd thought she was saved, thought she'd been thrown onto the riverbank.

When she'd lifted her head—everything else as limp as a noodle—she'd felt such a wave of despair that she might as well have been drowning.

She was trapped.

The water was too strong. Or she was too weak.

She couldn't swim to shore, not in this current.

Fear choked her. She laid her cheek on the ground, hot tears rolling down her cheeks.

She wasn't going to make it back to camp.

Sara was going to grow up without a mother, without a big sister to protect her.

Evangeline would never see Leo again.

And that's when she realized the water was rising. What had been lapping at her toes moments before now wetted her calves.

She scrambled to a sitting position, pulling her knees in to her chest. She watched in horror as inch after inch of the tiny little island disappeared deeper into the water.

Apparently, she hadn't completely given up. Some part of her had thought she would rest a bit and then fight to reach shore.

Somehow.

Lightning flashed overhead. Through the pouring rain she made out something moving quickly through the river. Toward her.

The flash of light had been too quick. She hadn't been able to see—had that been Leo?

No! It was too dangerous.

"Evie!"

But that was his dear voice, shouting to be heard above the noise of the river and the rain.

She scrambled to her feet. The spit of land was so small that she barely fit. Leo's horse wouldn't be able to stand up, not without knocking her into the water.

"Stretch out your arm!"

He was moving at such a fast clip that there wasn't time to think.

She didn't want to die out here.

So she leapt awkwardly toward him, her feet splashing in the icy water as she threw herself in his direction.

His arm clasped her waist like an iron band. She clung to his shoulders. Was he real? Had he really come for her, or was she dreaming?

Rivulets of rain ran off his hat and into her face, splattering her with cold water. That wasn't very dream-like.

The river pulled at her, but Leo held fast. He clung to the saddle with one hand and her with the other.

Lightning flashed again and illuminated the chiseled profile of his face, muddy and rain-spattered and oh, so dear.

And then something changed. The horse's front hooves must've hit the riverbank. For a moment, the water tried to drag her out of Leo's arms before he gained the saddle and pulled her onto his lap.

He guided the horse fully out of the river. Water streamed off of them, even as rain pelted them from above. When they'd made it to higher ground, Leo pulled the horse to a stop.

He dropped the reins and framed her face with his hands. "Are you all right?"

He didn't wait for her answer, only dropped his chin and kissed her. His lips were cool, chilled by the rain, but all she felt was warm and safe in his embrace.

"Please tell me—" Another kiss. "That you're all right."

"I don't know." Her voice shook, and she clasped his wrist with a trembling hand. She returned his kiss with fervor born from the terror she'd just experienced. "I think so."

He dropped his hands and hers fell away. He held her closer, trapping her arms between them as he kissed her cheek, her jaw.

"I saw you out on that spit and I couldn't breathe." He said the words against the sensitive skin just beneath her ear. "I didn't know whether you were alive or dead. I couldn't bear it if I lost you."

His words penetrated the haze of relief and affection overwhelming her. She went still as he pressed her closer, as he pressed kisses into the crown of her head.

When he tipped her head back with two fingers under her chin, clearly intent on kissing her mouth again, she pushed against his chest.

"Leo, stop."

He froze. Blinked at her. The warmth in his eyes didn't change, but she suddenly felt the coldness of wet cloth against her skin, the icy rain still pouring down.

"We shouldn't," she said.

"Why not?" He asked the question in his straightforward way. "Evie, when I saw you in the river, it couldn't have been more clear to me. I love you."

Her breath froze in her chest. Suddenly, the noise of the falling rain, the horse breathing beneath them, everything faded away in the roar of her heartbeat in her ears.

Leo loved her.

Or he thought he did.

She closed her eyes against the hope in his expression. "You don't love me. You can't. You don't even know me."

"Sure, I do."

He didn't understand.

"I've been lying to you the entire time we've known each other." She opened her eyes so he'd know she wasn't lying now. Willed him to believe the truth. "Sara isn't my sister. She's my daughter."

The words hung in the air between them. She saw the moment he understood, the minute change in his expression.

She had to tell him all of it.

"I fell in love with someone back in Boston. I believed all the promises he made me. I—I gave him my body when I knew I should wait until after we were married. He—he had been making promises to two other girls at the same time."

Saying the words brought a wave of betrayal that swept over her like the river had, tumbled her in the undertow.

She took a shuddering breath. "I know God has forgiven me, but I can't expect others to be as forgiving. I won't ever marry."

His jaw firmed stubbornly. "Evie, none of that changes how I feel."

She shook her head. Maybe not in this moment, when he was carried away by his passion. But once he realized what it meant, he would look at her differently. Treat her differently.

He opened his mouth to argue with her further, but a shout from behind him interrupted the moment.

Coop, riding toward them with her horse in tow and pushing the missing cow.

"You found the steer." Evangeline's relief brought tears to her eyes.

Or maybe that was the grief, loosened by everything that had led up to this moment.

Coop stopped to take in Evangeline's rumpled state, Leo's protective hand at her waist.

She couldn't look at Leo. Not now.

"The cow crossed the river and was hiding in a clump of plum trees. I never woulda seen her if I hadn't been after your horse. You all right?"

No. She never would be right again. But she nodded anyway, wiping beneath her nose with the heel of one wrist.

"Collin will be trying to send out a search party," Coop said. "We'd better get back."

She couldn't look at Leo again, so she turned her face to the side as they rode through the rain back to camp.

Twenty

LEO HELPED Evangeline off the horse when they arrived at camp. She was still soaking wet and, now that the rain had moved off, she would want to get dry. The clouds had shifted to the eastern horizon, and he could still see flashes of lightning occasionally, though the thunder was so distant it didn't register.

He wouldn't soon forget the terror of seeing her unmoving body in the middle of that river.

Neither would he forget the helplessness in her expression as she revealed her secret to him.

She had seemed almost relieved for Coop's interruption. As if she had said everything she needed to say and that was it.

But it wasn't finished for Leo.

How could she think his love for her was so weak? She'd been carrying a terrible secret for so long... He didn't agree with the lies she had told, but he understood. It was to protect her daughter. Maybe even to protect Evangeline herself.

She hurried off without a backward glance. That was all right. He had things to put in motion.

He took care of the horses, studiously ignoring Coop. He

still didn't know what his brother's distraction had been, the reason he'd lost track of that steer and Evangeline. He would have it out with Cooper later. For now, Evangeline was what mattered.

By the time he got to Alice's roaring fire between their two wagons, Evangeline had on a pale blue dress and a blanket wrapped around her shoulders as she sat close to the fire. Sara sat on her lap, and Alice fussed over her.

Her father stood near the wagon. Leo strode toward him.

"I need to speak to you. Can we take a walk?"

James looked at him pointedly. "You sure you don't want to put on something dry first? Evangeline told us you went out into the river to rescue her."

Leo shook his head. "It can't wait."

James nodded. Leo slowed his stride as they left the circle of the campfire. He had to remember the man still wasn't at his best, though he was much recovered. Leo turned to make a circuit around the outer edges of the circled wagons.

"I can't thank you enough for rescuing my daughter."

Leo shook his head. "I don't need any thanks for that. My fool brother..." He let his words trail off because his mind threw up an image of what it must've been like for that river bank to break away beneath Evangeline's horse. He didn't want to think about the danger she'd been in.

"I'm in love with your daughter."

Maybe he shouldn't have blurted it out like that, but he wasn't suave or well-spoken. He was just Leo.

James didn't even look surprised. "Have you told her that?"

"I have. I probably should've chosen a better time and place for it, though."

"She didn't take it well, I gather?" James squinted at the clouds on the far horizon. He put one hand to his ribs, an unconscious movement that showed Leo he was still hurting. He sighed. "I don't know if there would've been a right time and place."

"She told me about Sara's father."

Now the older man's expression registered shock.

Leo rushed on. "I don't care what happened in the past. I want to marry your daughter. I'd like your blessing, and it would help if you could talk to her. She has some misguided idea about never marrying."

James shook his head sadly. "I wish that my talking to her would make a difference. If only you could've known the Evangeline of three years ago. When she discovered she was with child, she came to me immediately. She was fearless. She had a plan for what she would do if I disowned her. I didn't, of course. After what that boy did to her, I thought she would be broken, but she didn't try to hide. She moved in society all the way up until the end. I'm ashamed to say I didn't talk to her as much as I should've. After Evangeline's mother died, things were... difficult. Laura always knew the right things to say. It was easier for me to focus on my business. I worried and fretted and kept it all to myself. And now she won't let me in." He sighed again. "I've got all the money in the world, but I'd give it all up to make her happy."

The two of them were a fine pair.

There was a sudden movement, a shadow changing shape near one of the wagons. Leo glanced over, but all seemed still in the darkness.

He scuffed his toe in the dirt.

"There's months still to go before we reach Oregon," James said. "You can change her mind. She cares for you."

Leo's heart leapt at the thought. He'd been so relieved to have her safe in his arms that he'd kissed her—and she'd kissed him back. Fervently. She'd clung to him like he was her rock, like she'd wanted to be in his arms.

Then she'd pushed him away, but she couldn't take back what had happened.

Leo felt a renewed determination. Evangeline deserved to have someone fight for her. Why not him?

"You won't stand in my way if I can convince her to marry me?"

James shook his head. "If you convince her to marry you, I will give you my blessing."

That was all Leo needed to hear.

* * *

Evangeline couldn't get warm.

Alice plied her with hot coffee and wrapped a second blanket tightly around her, but none of it seemed to help.

Not even Sara snuggling on her lap. The little girl was usually a furnace, most notably at night when she rolled over on Evangeline in their shared bed.

Maybe it had something to do with the secret she'd blurted out to Leo.

She hadn't been able to look at him since. She didn't want to see the recrimination or judgment in his expression. He had said that it didn't matter to him, but how could it not?

It didn't change anything. She had begun on this journey for one reason only. To make a better life for her daughter. She couldn't afford to become distracted now.

"I heard what happened." Owen appeared from the direction of his wagon. "You or Leo need anything?"

She opened her mouth, but the words wouldn't come, so she only shook her head.

Owen's expression was wreathed in concern. It made tears clog her throat. She hadn't meant for it to happen but somehow he had become a friend.

Her stomach twisted. Would Leo tell him? Leo claimed they weren't brothers, that their relationship wasn't real. But she didn't know how to trust him not to tell.

Owen seemed to understand that she didn't want to talk right now.

Sara bounced on her lap, happy for someone to pay her

attention. She babbled and reached for Owen, who took her easily into his arms.

"Isn't it past your bedtime?" He ruffled Sara's hair, his big arms easily holding her weight.

He said hello to Alice and then, "I wanted to check in with Leo before I take over as captain."

Alice spoke from inside her tent, where she was rolling out bedrolls. "He'll be relieved to be done with that."

Had it already been four weeks that they'd been on the trail? It seemed an age. And it seemed only days since she'd known the warmth of Leo's smile.

Sara wriggled to get down. Owen obliged her. She danced toward the fire before he scooped her back up.

"You really are ready for bed."

Leo and Father appeared out of the darkness. Had they gone off together? Evangeline didn't remember that.

"I'll tuck her in," Father said. He moved to take Sara from Owen. "Your young man needs to talk to you."

Evangeline's stomach dropped.

Leo strode straight toward her, and there was no escaping the intent look in his eyes.

"Can you spare a coupla minutes for me, Romeo?"

Leo's gaze didn't even flicker toward Owen.

"I don't think there's anything left to say," she whispered when Leo continued to ignore his brother.

"I have plenty to say. I'll say it in front of everybody, but I don't think you'd want that."

She stood up, tilting her chin away from him.

"Guess I'll come back later," Owen muttered.

She kept the blanket wrapped around her shoulders like a shawl and followed Leo out of the circle of light cast by the campfire. She stopped several paces beyond the tent, where she could hear her father speaking in low tones with Sara.

"I think we should get married."

She shivered. Surely she'd misheard him.

He went on, "I asked your father for his blessing, and he's given it."

Her brain felt as sluggish as her body had been trying to fight through that current. "Why would you ask my father that? I haven't given you any indication that I wanted to marry you."

"Your kisses said otherwise. I know you, Evangeline. You wouldn't have kissed me like that if you didn't feel anything for me."

Without her consent, the idea sank into her brain, sliding little tentacles like hooks into her heart as she imagined being Leo's wife. She ruthlessly pushed away the idea.

She threw up her hands in exasperation, the movement shifting the blanket off her shoulders. "I told you, my only concern is Sara. I don't want to get married. I don't—I don't deserve that kind of happiness." The rogue thought slipped from her mouth.

He had shifted closer to her, behind her shoulder but not touching her.

"You think you're the only one who's made mistakes? I thought I could keep Coop under control." His voice broke a little. "Back in New Jersey—at the powder mill—a man lost his life. Our family had to leave."

Her heart went out to him. He carried so much responsibility.

"I promised my mother that I'd do right by the boys, and I haven't." He paused. "Maybe I should've left Coop to face consequences back home, but I—"

He cut himself off. "You came west for a fresh start. We can have that. Together."

The idea took hold in her, deepening those tentacles with their deadly hooks.

"It would work." Had he seen the idea taking hold in her?

"You said you wanted adventure," she countered. "Will you leave Sara and I behind to go sail on your pirate ship?"

"Of course I wouldn't—"

She turned to face him in the dark, arms wrapped around her middle, barely holding onto herself. "Marrying me would be like yoking yourself to a wagon filled with boulders. You want freedom from being the one to take care of your family. How will that work? You resent Coop and what he's done to your family. You'd come to resent us, too."

He was silent. Maybe he was finally hearing her.

Suddenly, sounds of a scuffle came from nearby.

A muffled shout in the darkness, words spoken too low for her to understand.

Leo pushed her behind him, farther into the darkness, as a deafening gunshot roared.

Twenty-One

EVANGELINE KNELT NEXT to her father, holding her hands against the wound in his side.

She couldn't think—

Urgent male voices spoke in hushed tones somewhere in the periphery. And then Alice was there, pushing Evangeline's bare hands out of the way to press a cloth against Father's wound.

"We need to get Maddie." Her voice was shaky, but she staved off tears by sheer force of will. Father needed her now. She must be brave.

Thank goodness Sara was safe, sleeping in her tent. She sent a glance over her shoulder as if she could check on the girl merely with her eyes. There was a shadow in the darkness, hovering close to the tent. And then she registered that it was August, standing there to protect her daughter, or possibly to keep her away from this horrible tableau.

"Maddie is coming," Alice murmured.

Shouts rose from somewhere else in camp. Another gunshot, one that made Evangeline jump. A woman screamed.

And then it went silent, only the sounds of Father's labored breathing in the night.

His hand reached out to clasp hers. His skin was sticky with blood, his grip weak.

His lips moved, but the sound was so faint that Evangeline couldn't hear him.

She squeezed his hand in hers, leaning close to his face.

"I'm here," she whispered tearfully. "What did you say?"

"Maddie can't... save me." Every word cost him. They came stilted. He was obviously in pain.

Tears pricked her eyes. "Don't say that."

Light bobbed. A lantern cast yellow light on father's face. He was pale, lines of pain drawn around his mouth, but his eyes were steady. He stared at her face as if to memorize every feature.

"You've... always been... my... greatest... prize." His words grew fainter, and her heartbeat grew frantic.

"You don't have to speak," she whispered. A tear dripped off the end of her nose. When had it escaped? She hadn't noticed.

"My... prize," he whispered fiercely.

"Maddie will be here soon." She choked, barely holding back a sob.

He was fading away before her very eyes.

Leo crouched behind her, one big hand on her shoulder .

Father's gaze tracked to him, a fierce light in his eyes. "Don't let them... take Evie's money."

Money? Had he been shot because of their money?

"Take... care... of her."

"I will," Leo said solemnly.

She shook her head as further tears threatened. She didn't want that. Didn't want him to give her over to Leo.

Alice slipped her arm around Evangeline's waist. Why wasn't she pressing the towel against Father? Evangeline spared a glance but couldn't register the blood soaking through the towel at his side and spilling on the ground.

Father squeezed her hand painfully tight, ripping her attention back to him. His breathing was so quiet now she couldn't hear it. She leaned as close as she dared.

"Don't... build... a life... for Sara."

Instant refusal rose to her lips even though she couldn't make her sluggish brain work. Why would he say such a thing?

"Do it... for you."

Air hissed through his lips and his head lolled to the side, his eyes now empty and lifeless.

"No." On the heels of the single word, a sob burst from her lips.

"Evie—"

She couldn't bear Leo's touch. Not now. She dropped her father's lifeless hand to brush Leo's from her shoulder.

She bent in half, her forehead almost touching the ground as sobs wracked her. Alice's arms closed around her. Evangeline didn't fight her friend's embrace.

She couldn't think, couldn't stop the terrible sobs that tried to rip her in half.

Only one word played over and over in her mind. No.

No.

No.

No.

Father couldn't be gone. It couldn't be possible.

But the gaping hole inside her assured her that it was.

* * *

Leo stood by, helpless, as Evangeline sobbed over her father's dead body.

She had pushed him away.

He couldn't fault her, not in this moment when she was grieving so desperately.

At least she allowed Alice close. His sister whispered to Evangeline, offered comforting words with strokes down her hair. Evangeline needed someone, and if all she could accept right now was Alice, he would be happy for that.

But anger boiled behind the helpless feeling. Why had this happened? And who had done it?

His anger needed a target.

Coop was nowhere to be seen, and Owen had gone chasing after whoever had been shooting. Maddie had come and gone. Apparently, someone else had needed her. And there was nothing to be done for James now.

Collin and Leo were left to watch over Evangeline and her father while August was keeping an eye on Sara's tent. Each man was armed. Leo knew Evangeline wouldn't want her daughter to see this. For one moment, he was thankful for his half brothers.

Don't let them... take Evie's money. Whoever had shot James in cold blood might've been after the money Evangeline had told him about, the gold coins stashed in a hidden compartment in their wagon.

There was movement near the campfire, but whoever was there was hidden from Leo's sight.

Was the man or men who'd done this back? Leo glanced at Collin, who'd noticed someone, too. Leo nodded to Evangeline and Alice. Collin's mouth pulled in a straight line. He would watch over them.

Leo snuck around the back of the wagon, keeping his footsteps muffled in the prairie grass. He paused when he heard a sound like paper tearing. Drew his gun. Held it at the ready as he stepped around the wagon.

And found Coop, shoulders turned toward the wagon, standing where no one could see him unless they were close. He had one hand over his eyes. Was he...? He was crying, Leo realized. Almost silently.

Terrible foreboding shot through Leo.

He was upset. Hurting. He'd admired James. They were friends. He also bore an echoing hurt, knowing how Evangeline must be feeling right now.

But his eyes were dry, while Coop's weren't.

His anger surged.

"What did you do?" The words rumbled out of Leo, low and dangerous. He shoved his revolver into its holster at his waist.

Coop's hand fell away from his face and, sure enough, his eyes were red-rimmed and bloodshot.

"I didn't—" Coop's voice broke, and he took another of those shuddering breaths.

Leo shook his brother by his shoulders. "What did you do?"

Coop didn't push back against Leo's shove. "I didn't shoot James."

But there was guilt written on Coop's expression.

Leo's anger went white-hot. "You didn't pull the trigger? But you were involved. Or you know who did. Which is it?"

Lost in his righteous anger, Leo shoved his brother again. Coop fell against the wagon, the entire conveyance shaking. Coop didn't fight back, just looked at Leo with a lost expression.

Leo could still hear the sound of Evangeline's sobs in the quiet of night, and because his woman was hurting, his instinct was to raise his arm and ready for a punch.

"Leo." Owen's voice broke through his single-minded thought—hurt Coop the way Evangeline was hurting. Leo's arm trembled with the urge to throw his fist. Coop wasn't defending himself. From this close, Leo might shatter his brother's jaw.

"Not now." Owen's voice was low and reasonable, and the last thing Leo wanted to do was listen to it.

"Evangeline needs you. If you knock out your brother, I'm going to have to tie you up until we get all this sorted out."

Leo blinked. That's right. He wasn't captain anymore. Today, Owen had taken over that job.

And Owen had said the one thing that could break

through Leo's anger towards his brother. Evangeline needed him.

He took a half step back, dropped his arm to his side.

Coop turned his face away.

"He knows some thing," Leo told Owen. "Or he did something."

"I've got another man shot and one missing," Owen said. "I could use your help."

Leo glanced toward Evangeline, but the wagon hid her from sight. Her sobs had tapered off, and he could hear Alice speaking to her.

"You don't even want to hear what I have to say?" Coop asked in a voice laced with hurt.

Leo didn't look at his brother.

"As far as I'm concerned, you've brought this mess on yourself. I'm done cleaning up after you." Leo tipped his head toward Owen. "Owen is the captain now. Whatever punishment he metes out is what you'll get." To Owen, he said, "Let me check on Evangeline and then I'll help you."

He strode out into the darkness. But he didn't immediately go to Evangeline. Collin crouched next to the two women as he spoke softly.

Collin had turned into an exceptional young man. Alice was the glue that kept all of them together.

Where had he gone wrong with Coop?

Promise me.

He could still hear his mother's last whispered plea, begging him to keep the family together, to take care of her sons.

"Leo—"

Coop's voice rang out behind him, but Leo ignored him.

You resent Coop. Evangeline couldn't have known how true she'd spoken.

Leo remembered the little boy who'd looked up to him. Who'd put on Leo's boots and stumbled around their tenement, wanting to be just like his big brother.

That person didn't exist anymore.

For the first time in his life, Leo left his brother behind and didn't look back.

Twenty-Two

IT WAS ALMOST DAWN. Leo's shoulders ached from the repetitive motion of digging James's grave, but he kept at it.

At first, Collin had helped him. After a while, Owen and August had come to relieve them. Finally, Leo had told them he needed to finish this himself.

In less than an hour, Evangeline was going to have to say goodbye to her father, right there by the side of the trail.

Leo had spoken to Hollis, asked whether they could delay the wagon train's departure for a few hours, give a proper funeral. Time for Evangeline to grieve.

But Hollis insisted that today's leg wasn't one that could afford a delay. He'd give an extra half hour before the bugle rang but that was all he could do.

It wasn't enough.

Leo finally put down his shovel. A fine mist gathered inches above the ground as the sun peeked above the horizon with its first bright rays.

He felt so inadequate. How could he help Evangeline through this? He'd never been good with Alice's tears.

He was also aware that Evangeline hadn't given him an answer to his proposal. She'd only listed all the reasons they shouldn't be married.

Last night, she'd asked Alice to be with her as they'd washed James's body to prepare it for the burial.

She would be grieving today, crying. Maybe raging. She had a right. He would do everything he could to comfort her and care for her today.

But when a handful of folks gathered in the early dawn, Evangeline was silent. She barely looked at Leo as August, Collin, and Owen carried her father's body, wrapped in a sheet, then set it gently in the tear in the ground that Leo and his brothers had created.

Evangeline held Sara in her arms, Alice on one side of her, Leo on the other. Should he reach out? He wanted to clasp her hand in comfort, but her arms were around Sara. What if he put his arm around her?

Hollis started speaking before Leo decided. The man read a Psalm Leo had never heard of before, words of loss and sorrow.

Someone started singing "Amazing Grace." Slowly, other voices joined. When the final verse began, Leo felt his eyes prick with tears. But when he glanced at Evangeline, she was pale and dry-eyed.

Had she cried all her tears? Her stoicism worried him.

After the service was over, Leo's brothers picked up the pair of shovels and began filling in the grave.

Evangeline moved a few yards away and stood as folks came to give their condolences. The sound of the shovel *slicing* into the freshly turned dirt and the echo when the loose earth rained into the grave seemed so final.

Leo followed Evangeline, stood next to her, but she never looked at him.

His stomach went sour.

The sun kept rising. Time was running short. The sounds of camp pulling out slowly came into focus.

Sara started to get restless. Alice murmured to Evangeline before she took the girl and moved back toward the wagon.

Steven Fairfax was last to leave. Then it was only Evangeline and Leo and the awful sounds of the shovels moving dirt.

"Have you eaten breakfast?" Leo asked.

"I'm not hungry."

Her words were so matter of fact that they made Leo want to argue with her. She needed to eat if she wanted to keep her strength up. But he didn't say that.

"I'll be driving your wagon today," he said. "It should be fine if you and Sara want to ride inside. You should rest." He knew she'd been up all night.

She stared ahead, her expression giving away nothing.

And then she seemed to come to some decision. She turned toward him, though she still didn't look him in the eye. "I'll drive our wagon today. Sara can ride with me."

She sounded calm and businesslike. But she'd only driven the wagon once, and only for an hour or so. She couldn't mean it.

He knew she'd had a terrible shock, still hadn't processed what had happened. "Evie, we had a deal. I'll drive."

"Don't call me that." Her voice sharpened.

He reached for her then, one hand extended to touch her arm, but she turned her body away from him so that his hand only met air.

She inhaled once, the sound slightly ragged. "There is no deal. Not anymore."

He knew this wasn't the best timing. She needed rest.

But he couldn't seem to stop the words falling from his mouth, "Sweetheart, we never finished our conversation last night."

"There's nothing left to say." She sounded so defeated.

"Everything's changed now," he said. *You're all alone.* He wanted to give her his protection. "Marriage is the sensible option."

Her chin jerked up. "Nothing about it is sensible. My answer is no."

She wouldn't listen. It made his temper flash. "You're right. There isn't a deal anymore. I'm giving you back the money you paid me."

She turned on him, eyes flashing. "You can't. You need that money for when your family arrives in Oregon."

He shook his head. "I'm not taking your money. I'm not interested in a business deal. I want your heart."

Now her eyes flashed again, an unhappy frown appearing. She shook her head slowly.

His heart dipped. "Evie—Evangeline, your heart is so big. I see how much you love Sara. Just let me in."

She firmed her lips. "Stop telling me what to do. I know my own mind. I'm not your sister."

He flinched at the harshness of her words.

When she turned her face away, he saw the stubborn set of her jaw.

This wasn't right, he was making a hash of this.

"I don't want your help anymore, Leo." Her words rang with finality. "If I can't handle the wagon, I'll ask Owen or Steven Fairfax to spell me." *Anyone but you.*

"Why are you being so stubborn?" he demanded.

"Why are you?" she countered. "You want freedom. Adventure. Now's your chance to have it."

Not like this. He hadn't wanted this.

Promise me.

You resent Coop.

Two loved voices warred in his head. His heart was bruised from losing James and from everything that had happened in the past twenty-four hours.

Evangeline didn't want him. How many times did she have to say it before he believed her?

"Fine," he spat. "Good luck to you."

He walked away without looking back.

* * *

Leo stood with his arms crossed, away from the restless group of men.

After a long day of travel, everyone was weary. Leo even more so after a night spent without sleep while digging James's grave.

But Hollis and Owen, acting as captain, had called for a meeting of all of the men in camp. It was set to start any minute now. The men had gathered near a clump of tall trees.

Leo had spent the day driving the wagon with Owen's prisoner in it. He hadn't had the heart to ask if it was Coop inside the wagon with its tightly closed flaps. He hadn't seen his brother amidst the traveling wagons or riders on horseback. He'd felt nauseated all day, no appetite.

At least driving a different wagon meant he hadn't had to ride close to Evangeline.

He felt raw, like a wound scraped open.

Someone sidled up next to him, even though Leo was broadcasting *stay away from me* through his stance. He glanced over.

Coop.

A thread of relief laced through his confusing tangle of emotions. If Coop wasn't inside that wagon, then he wasn't the man Owen had chased down last night.

Leo didn't say a word.

Coop shifted his feet.

"You're not even going to talk to me?"

Leo didn't answer.

"You don't want to know whether or not I was involved?"

Leo couldn't bear his brother's presence right now. He was too raw, his emotions too close to the surface.

"I overheard you and Evangeline talking that first night. I knew about your plan and her money the whole time."

He had? Leo couldn't help wondering if she had been in danger all this time.

"I didn't tell anybody. At least, I don't think I did."

"What does that mean?" Leo ground out.

Coop shifted restlessly again. "There was one night I was..."

"Getting roostered," Leo spat bitterly. There was no use skirting around the truth.

Coop sighed. "I was drinking with a couple of friends. I went a little overboard and the next morning, I couldn't remember much."

"So you could've told them." Leo had never been that out of control before. He couldn't imagine the terror of waking up and not knowing where he'd been. Who he had been with. What he had done.

"Neither of my friends were involved. I already spoke to Owen."

Leo's lips twisted. "How can you call men like that your friends? They're just using you. And when you're not useful to them anymore, they'll be finished with you."

Coop bristled. "You don't know—"

Leo cut him off with a slice of his hand through the air.

Hollis stepped to the front of the gathered group of men. Beside him stood Owen and Philip, the young man who had been caught stealing money, along with his cousin Tony.

"This isn't a trial," Hollis said, his voice grave. "There were witnesses who heard Philip admit to his uncle that he shot James. When his uncle tried to get him to turn himself in to me, he shot Eric, too. Eric passed away this afternoon from the wound in his gut."

There were whispers among some of the men, but they didn't last long.

Leo had sensed the teen was unrepentant about the theft. They were only two days from Fort Kearny. Had the boy become desperate, this close to being left behind, left to fend for himself?

Leo'd purposely kept himself separated from everyone today, needing space to lick his wounds, try to get his head on straight. He hadn't heard any gossip; so this was a complete surprise.

The boy looked just as unrepentant now. He spat on the ground in front of him. "My uncle deserved what he got."

"You knew the consequences," Hollis said. "It's time for you to face your punishment."

Owen put the young man up on horseback while Clarence secured his neck in a noose hanging from a tree limb. Philip stared ahead, stone-faced.

Leo couldn't watch. When he looked away, he caught sight of Coop, his face chalk white, eyes glued to what was happening.

Leo looked down at his feet. He felt numb. No hope that Coop would change, no more sense of responsibility. He'd washed his hands of Coop.

Even the things he'd said moments ago had been more out of habit than out of a sense of duty.

When it was over, folks dispersed, silent and sad.

The young man had murdered two people and gotten what he deserved. But the justice felt hollow. Nothing would bring back James or Eric.

Leo distanced himself from Coop, choosing to walk the long way around instead of going with his brother. When he got back to camp, Alice and Collin were there, speaking in quiet voices.

Alice had tears on her cheeks. Leo felt empty, but he moved to put his arm around her.

"I can't do it anymore," he said, voice rough. "I can't be the one to keep Coop in line."

Collin had his head bowed where he sat on his saddle near the fire. "Mama should've never asked you what she did."

Alice pushed away from Leo, wiping her face. "It wasn't right. Wasn't fair. You were just a child yourself."

Maybe she was right, but who had ever said that life was supposed to be fair?

Leo had tried and tried, but he couldn't do it anymore.

Maybe that made him just as selfish as the father who had walked away when Leo had been small.

Maybe Leo was more like the man than he'd ever thought.

Twenty-Three

THREE DAYS HAD PASSED since Evangeline's whole world had crumbled. Evening was falling and she and Sara had traipsed away from camp to wash laundry in a little creek.

She hadn't meant to come so far, but everything inside had risen to choke her and she'd had to keep going until she felt she could breathe.

That's where Alice found her. At a little bend in the creek, hunched over a metal and wood washboard, scrubbing soap into dirty clothes. Sara waded in the water a few yards away.

"It's gettin' kind of dark." Alice's voice made Evangeline jump. Her knuckles rapped against the washboard, and she hissed in a breath at the stinging pain.

"I'm almost done," she said. With this chore. There was much left to do back in camp, including preparing wood for a fire for breakfast and pitching the tent.

She hadn't realized how completely she'd leaned on Leo and his family until now, when she was determined to finish this journey on her own.

Her shoulders ached from holding her arms *just so* and

fighting the reins all day. She'd scratched her cheek and nearly gotten stepped on when she'd unhitched the oxen tonight.

Exhaustion made her want to cry.

She knew she couldn't.

"Did you mean to come so far from camp?" Alice asked casually. "And to park your wagon so far from ours?"

It had taken quite a bit of maneuvering to get another wagon between hers and the one Collin drove. Then the Earlywine's wagon had stopped completely thanks to a broken wheel. Two other wagons had slowed to check if the older couple needed help. Evangeline had snapped the reins and slipped ahead of them in the snaking line of wagons.

She'd wanted the space.

She hadn't planned for the hurt in Alice's voice.

Hearing it made an answering ache in the pit of her stomach.

"I just drove the wagon, Alice."

Her old friends back in Boston would've never questioned the white lie. They would've smiled to her face and said what they wanted behind her back.

But Alice wasn't like those young women. She leaned down and splashed water from the creek right at Evangeline.

"Hey!" Evangeline sputtered as droplets of water hit her torso and face. It didn't matter, not really. She was already damp from her washing.

It was the principal of the thing.

But Evangeline didn't splash back. She only bent over her washing and kept scrubbing. She couldn't muster the energy for anything else.

Alice stood with hands on her hips. She hiked her chin toward Sara. "Did you really think tying her skirt up like that would keep her dry?"

"I really did." Evangeline had tucked Sara's skirt into her pantaloons, thinking that only her feet would get wet.

But the first thing Sara had done was fallen in the water and soaked her whole body. She'd squealed with delight.

Evangeline had hidden her dismay. One more thing to clean and dry.

With Father gone, it seemed the work was never ending. But it still wasn't enough for her to forget the grief.

Those pesky tears threatened again, hot and painful behind her nose.

All of this was her fault. Her fault.

Alice stood there. Maybe she was waiting for Evangeline to say something. Evangeline switched to one of Father's shirts and scrubbed it with vigor. What was she going to do with it now? She had no use for it.

Alice could wait all she wanted. Evangeline had nothing to say. If she didn't let the feelings in, they didn't exist.

Alice did wait.

Much longer than was polite.

Finally, she threw up her hands in exasperation. "Are you going to stop being my friend because my stupid brother said the wrong thing?"

Thinking of Leo sharpened the pain in Evangeline's chest.

The thought of losing Alice's friendship made it worse. Emotions leaked inside her suddenly cracked heart.

Evangeline knocked her knuckles again, this time drawing blood. She shook out her hand, dipped it in the creek.

Her fault.

"I don't want your friendship," Evangeline said. She even sounded as if she meant it.

"Liar."

Liar, liar.

Sara was still splashing around, not paying them any attention.

"Tell me what's truly going on," Alice demanded.

The words burst out of Evangeline before she could stop them. "I c-can't be your friend. Everything that's happened is my fault."

Alice's voice was quiet and firm. "James's death wasn't your fault."

Evangeline clutched the sopping wet fabric in her hands, head bowed. "Father came west because of me."

"He came because he wanted to. He loved you."

My prize.

Her father had called her that in his dying words. The reminder burst through the last of her walls holding her grief in. Tears choked her, but she refused to let them out.

Her relationship with Father had been broken for a long time. She'd carried the guilt of her sins, kept him at a distance.

"Leo loves you, too," Alice said determinedly, the words breaking into Evangeline's thoughts. "Whatever he said—that morning, well, he didn't mean it."

"He can't love me." Evangeline scrubbed harder. Hard enough that her fingers hurt.

"Why not? You love him."

"No, I don't." If Alice would only leave her alone. If she scrubbed hard enough, the tears pricking her eyes would go away.

"Yes, you do. You sing during chores after he compliments your breakfast. You make sure he gets the largest serving at supper. You listen outside the tent to the bedtime stories he tells Sara."

She did do all of that, but... Evangeline shook her head. "None of that means I love Leo."

Alice hopped the creek at a narrow spot so she was on the same side as Evangeline.

"Yes, you do."

Stubborn girl.

"I want to hear you admit it."

"I can't. Because it isn't true."

Alice let out a very unladylike growl. "You light up when he looks at you. Say it."

Evangeline shook her head again.

"If you don't admit to it, I'll... I'll push you in the creek."

She really didn't see why Alice was getting so worked up

over three silly words. Yes, Leo was special, but she *couldn't* love him.

"Alice, I don't lo—"

Evangeline didn't get the words out before she was unceremoniously shoved between her shoulder blades, toppling forward. She windmilled her arms but there was nothing to catch her.

She tumbled into the water. What had been cool on her hands was a shock to her entire body. She gasped, water flooding her mouth.

She found her feet and stood, water running off her in rivulets, spluttering.

"Alice! How could you—?"

"Say it," Alice demanded. She looked so fierce, her eyes flashing with emotion.

Evangeline turned her head. Sara was stock still, mouth open, several yards downstream. A tiny speck of white floated toward her daughter on the current.

"My soap is floating away," she said petulantly to Alice.

Who looked even more stubborn. "Say it."

"I love Leo," Evangeline burst out.

Alice looked surprised, but not as surprised as Evangeline was to realize her friend was right.

She burst into tears and covered her face with both hands, which was ridiculous because Alice had already seen.

Alice said something quiet to Sara. Then there was splashing. Too much for the little girl to be making alone.

More splashing.

And then Alice's arms came around her.

Evangeline's tears had already dried to an occasional hiccup. She'd cried all night the night father had died. How could there be any more tears?

"I can't love Leo," she whispered into Alice's shoulder.

She took a step back, water swirling around her calves. Alice had come into the water just to comfort her.

"I've made so many mistakes," she said on a hiccup.

"Everyone makes mistakes."

Leo had said the same thing. She'd told herself she was made new, that God had forgiven her, but she hadn't really believed it.

She hadn't forgiven herself.

She didn't know if she could.

Alice sat with her for a long time.

"I know it's frightening to love someone," Alice said finally.

"You do?"

"It must be. You're trusting that they won't break your heart." She paused. "Leo is very trustworthy."

Evangeline exhaled softly. "I know."

"So what will you do about it?"

That was the one thing Evangeline didn't know.

* * *

"You make up with Coop yet?"

Leo had been aware of the approaching horse. Night had fallen not long ago, and he was on watch. He had hoped to have a quiet night, but when he heard Owen's question, he figured it was a lost cause.

"You goin' to?" Owen asked when he hadn't answered.

"Was there something you needed?" Because Leo needed Owen to stop. Leo didn't want to be reminded of Coop's expression as he'd watched that boy take his punishment. Coop had looked... lost.

Leo had spent days trying not to think about it. Or Evangeline.

Alice and Collin had told him that Coop wasn't his responsibility, but that hadn't stopped them from trying to keep the peace. Alice had mentioned to Leo no more than five times how Coop was in camp well before curfew and doing all his chores without having to be reminded.

And now she must've recruited Owen.

Leo was a little surprised that his half brother had agreed to do it.

"How's Evangeline?" Owen's change of subject made Leo flinch. He tried to hide it by turning his head to scan the opposite horizon.

"You know better than I do," Leo said bitterly.

Owen had been welcomed into Evangeline's campsite. He had sat with her at breakfast this morning, huddled close to her fire to ward off the chill. Jealousy had churned in Leo's stomach, and he'd had to take a walk. He couldn't watch them together.

Even though he'd been the one to walk away from her. Just like he had Coop.

"She's not saying much."

A twisted kind of gratification bled through Leo. If Evangeline wasn't talking to him, at least she wasn't talking to Owen either.

He had to work at keeping his hand relaxed on the reins. Owen was obviously trying to get some kind of reaction out of him. Leo didn't know why.

"She's got to be torn up about what happened to her Pa."

It was hard to keep emotion from his face when he thought about what Evangeline was going through.

"August and I were in bad shape after Pa died."

Leo inhaled sharply through his nose, the breath stinging. He turned on Owen, still in the saddle, words falling hotly from his lips. "I wouldn't know about that, would I? He left us."

"You mean like you did to Coop?"

It was easier to talk about Coop than think about his father and the big gaping wound in Leo's heart. One that he'd thought had been scarred over for two decades.

"I can't keep going the way things have been," Leo said.

"Nobody's saying you have to. Maybe it'll be good for him to have a shakeup."

Or maybe he'd get himself in such deep trouble he couldn't get out.

"He's your family," Owen said. "Not a noose around your neck. You can love him and still be angry. That's what I felt toward Pa."

Leo was surprised to hear that.

"I would've liked to have known you," Owen admitted.

Now past surprised, Leo was taken aback. "You... would?"

"Of course. Why do you think August and I came along?"

"All this time, I thought it was about you making amends on Pa's behalf."

Owen scoffed. "You think I'd put up with your terrible attitude for months because of Pa?"

Leo took a moment to come to terms with what his brother had revealed. Why hadn't Owen ever said something before?

Probably because Leo'd pushed him away from the moment they'd met. Leo hadn't wanted anything to do with the two brothers who'd looked and sounded just like the pa who'd abandoned him.

Owen spoke, all the teasing gone from his voice. "He regretted it at the end. Leaving you and Alice. He told me so himself those last days. Said he'd worked himself to the bone to keep from thinking about you."

For the first time, Leo felt a pang of something that wasn't anger or bitterness toward his father.

Why had Pa left if he'd loved them? Missed them?

Maybe Owen didn't have the answers. Maybe Leo would never get them.

But did he really want to spend the rest of his life hating a man who was dead and buried?

"You remind me of him, sometimes," Owen said quietly.

Leo scowled in the darkness. "I'm not like him."

The words rang hollow.

Owen was sharp enough to recognize it, but he didn't say anything.

Leo had walked away from Coop. Walked away from Evangeline too.

"She pushed me away." He didn't know who was more surprised by his gruff statement, him or Owen.

"You mean the morning after her father died? We both know she wasn't thinking straight."

She'd had enough presence of mind to cut him with words like swords.

Had he hurt her the same way? Neither one of them had slept that unending night. He couldn't even remember everything he'd said to her, though her words were burned into his brain.

"Don't make the same mistake Pa did," Owen said after a long hesitation on Leo's part.

"She doesn't want me." Saying the words out loud was like a knife ripping through his insides, spilling his pain all over again.

Owen focused on him. "Are you sure about that? Are you sure she's not just scared? Same as you are?"

Leo wanted to snap at his brother—but was Owen right? Evangeline had had her heart broken once before. She'd come west to make things better for Sara, expecting nothing for herself. No joy, only duty.

"It's complicated," he said finally.

"So uncomplicate it."

Owen wanted him to fight for her, but it wasn't that easy. Was it?

Leo cleared his throat. "For what it's worth, I'm glad to know you and August. Glad to call you brother."

"Took you long enough." Owen's smile came through in his voice in the darkness.

Twenty-Four

EVANGELINE STOOD at the edge of the river, staring out over the fast-moving, dark water. The Evangeline of a few weeks ago would've known which branch of which river she was looking at.

She hadn't opened one of her guidebooks in weeks. After everything the Mason family had taught her, Alice and Leo and Coop and Collin, she'd been living the things she'd once only read about.

The sun wasn't quite up yet and the pre-dawn gray made the waters look darker, more menacing.

She was supposed to cross this river today. She didn't know how to drive the wagon across water, to keep the conveyance afloat and keep an eye on Sara, keep them both from tumbling into the dangerous current.

Her own memories of the ground falling away beneath her, plunging into the water, the current ripping at her clothing and skin... were too close.

She felt as if she were trapped underwater, unable to breathe.

And then she heard footsteps behind her.

She turned to face the danger, one hand going to the pocket of her dress, where she'd stashed the derringer Owen had given her. Now that everyone on the wagon train knew she was traveling with money, she had to be constantly alert.

Leo walked straight toward her with unerring stride, something held loosely in one hand.

A book, she registered as he came closer.

She blushed, unable to conceal the feelings that bubbled up in her chest as she remembered Alice submerging her in that icy creek.

Leo wasn't a figment of her imagination. He was real, tall and broad-shouldered, his piercing blue gaze fixed on her.

"Morning, Evie."

She swallowed hard. "Hi."

"I need you to do something for me."

He did? Her pulse beat in her ears, threatening to drown out every other sound. "What is it?"

He stopped a couple of feet away from her and extended the book. "I want you to read this. Out loud. To me."

She scrunched her nose up as she took the book from him. It was one of her trail guides.

"I borrowed it from your stash of books," he admitted when she looked up at him questioningly.

It was hard to tell in the low light. Was *he* blushing? "I need you to read me the part about today's river crossing."

This was what he wanted to talk to her about? Disappointment tasted bitter in the back of her throat.

After missing him so desperately, after Alice's lecture and Evangeline's realization... well, she'd pictured the next time she would see Leo. Imagined being bold enough to tell him just how she felt, dreamed how he'd draw her close to him... maybe kiss her again.

Not this. Not *read to me*.

She opened her mouth to simply blurt it all out. *I love you. I'm sorry.*

But when she looked up at him, his gaze was fixed on the water behind her and she chickened out.

She flipped the book open, turned pages until she found the right description.

She couldn't keep her mind from racing, even as she read the passage with only half-attention.

Determination swelled inside her. She needed to tell him how she felt.

"That part," he interrupted gently. "Read that part again."

She blinked and re-focused on the words in front of her. "The crossing is wide and shallow, much less dangerous than what we traversed four days ago."

She felt the words settle inside her. Today's crossing still wouldn't be easy. There was a lot that could go wrong. But she didn't have to worry about a strong current sweeping the wagon away.

Leo had wanted her to know, she realized suddenly. That's why he'd insisted she read the passage to him. He wanted her to know she could handle the crossing without putting herself in danger.

He meant to comfort her.

Love swelled inside her.

"Would you ride in the wagon with me today?" She first aimed the question at the open pages of her book, but she was more courageous than that. By the end of her question she had dropped her hands and raised her chin to look him in the eye.

There was a beat of silence. Behind her, she could hear the sounds of camp coming to life.

"You don't need me to drive your wagon across," he said gently.

He was right. But he was looking at her so tenderly. And he was wrong, too.

"I do need you," she said quietly. There was a freedom in

saying the words, a relief that flowed through her whole body. "Someone has to ensure Sara doesn't jump out to try and swim across."

A slow smile spread across his lips.

"She's missed you," Evangeline admitted. "I have, too."

Some invisible tension seemed to drain from him. He reached for her. She came into his arms easily, accepting his embrace, tucking her head beneath his chin.

This felt right.

Someone called his name from a distance, and she started slightly. This wasn't the time for declarations, she realized.

There were too many people about. Someone needed Leo's help.

And surely Sara was awake and bothering Maddie. Evangeline had asked the young woman to keep an eye on the tent where Sara slept, in case the girl woke earlier than usual.

Leo seemed loathe to let her go, and that made it a little easier to leave his embrace.

Whoever had called his name did it again. Louder this time.

His smile was crooked. "I've got to see what he needs. I'll meet you at your wagon in a few minutes."

"All right."

He was true to his word. He joined her as she was hitching the oxen into their traces. When her arms shook with the weight of the yoke, he came beside her and joined his strength to hers.

A sense of rightness settled over her. She was meant to be at Leo's side.

"Lee!" Sara cried out from behind the wagon bench. Evangeline had settled her there with several wooden blocks, hoping to keep her occupied and away from dangerous hooves.

"Hello, peanut," he called out. "Can I ride across the river with you today?"

"Yay!" Sara sing-songed something else that Evangeline

couldn't make out and ducked through the flaps and into the wagon. Evangeline was glad she'd tied the back flap tightly. She didn't think Sara could wiggle her way through the jumble of boxes and barrels to fall out.

Leo moved to the opposite side of the oxen from Evangeline and mirrored her movements as she put the pins through the bow.

Every time she glanced up, he was watching her with an enigmatic smile.

She moved around the wagon, checking every tie and making sure it was as waterproof as she could make it.

She met Leo at the rear of the wagon. He opened his mouth as if he wanted to say something, but the bugle blew. It was time to move out.

She followed Leo to the front of the wagon. He handed her up into the seat. Sara popped her head up between their shoulders as Leo sat down. His leg pressed against Evangeline's on the narrow seat.

When she tried to hand Leo the reins, he held up his hand to stop her.

"You're capable," he reminded her. "I'm just here to occupy Sara."

He winked at her.

She urged the oxen into line behind another wagon, butterflies tickling her insides as Leo regaled Sara with a story of hearing coyotes howling last night on watch.

At the press of his thigh against hers on the seat, she drew a shuddering breath.

This might be a mistake. Her heart fluttered in her chest and anticipation made every nerve ending sing.

Maybe she should've blurted out her feelings to Leo earlier, then she would be able to concentrate.

The wagon in front of her splashed into the water and Evangeline flinched. Terrifying memories lurched to the front of her brain, but Leo's calm voice pulled her out of them.

"Your mama is a good driver," Leo said to Sara. "She's not going to let you go swimming today."

Somehow, Evangeline's white-knuckled grip on the reins brought them out into the water.

The guidebook had been right. It was shallow and slow.

She started to breathe again as Leo kept talking, now telling Sara about a litter of kittens someone on the wagon train had.

"Now she's going to want one," she warned him, her voice only slightly breathless with fear.

She could hear the smile in his voice. "So we'll get her one. It'll be good for keeping the mice out of your mill in Oregon."

He said the words so easily, as if he had no doubt that she would accomplish it.

She glanced at him—a split second look—and saw his steady, unwavering belief in her.

And she was able to relax her hands on the reins.

* * *

Evening shadows fell after the wagons had circled up.

Fires were lit and savory smells rose from cookpots all over camp.

After the river crossing, Leo had been called away by Hollis to help a family who'd lost some supplies in the river. He'd been on horseback ever since, disappointed that they hadn't had time to finish their conversation.

She's missed you. I have, too.

Evangeline's admission had kept him going all day. He'd been so hopeful, anticipating seeing her again, thinking how they might finish their conversation, that his horse had sensed his excitement and danced beneath him. More than once.

He was relieved to see her wagon parked back where it belonged—right next to the one he shared with his siblings.

Owen and August's wagon was there, too, on the other

side of Evangeline's. Leo felt only gratefulness, not caged-in the way he once would've.

The family campfire was busy.

Coop was inhaling food from a tin plate while standing near the wagon.

Collin and August had a checkerboard between them where they lounged on the ground, but Sara was moving pieces willy nilly. Both men watched her with patient smiles.

Alice had one foot off the ground, the other balanced on a spoke of the wagon wheel, leaning up into the conveyance as if she was searching for something.

Evangeline stood over the cookpot, though her attention was focused on Owen, who stood nearby. They were chatting, and what once would've filled Leo to the brim with jealousy didn't anymore.

Especially not when Evangeline caught his approach and smiled at him like she'd been waiting to see him all day.

He almost did it. He almost strode over to her and swept her into his arms, uncaring that his family was watching. They all knew how he felt about her. He'd done such a poor job of keeping his feelings to himself, and they'd all suffered for it.

But he didn't want to embarrass Evangeline.

And there was one niggling voice in the back of his head telling him that she could still change her mind about him. She'd said she missed him, not that she wanted him around for the next forty or fifty years.

"You mind washing that for me?" Coop spoke quietly to Collin and Leo's attention shifted to his brothers.

Coop sat his empty plate on the ground near Collin. "I've got first watch. Supposed to report to Hollis."

"All right," Collin said.

Coop tipped his hat to the rest of them before making his way out of the circle of wagons and into the darkness beyond.

He realized he was staring after his brother when Evangeline stepped up beside him. She had a plate full of venison stew in one hand and wore a tentative smile.

"You ready for supper? Alice cooked," she added when he took too long to answer.

He was too busy taking her in. Overwhelmed with gladness she was here.

"I like your cooking," he said.

She blushed a little, clearly pleased.

He took the plate and put it on the floorboard of her wagon, the closest place in reach. It'd save. "But I'm not hungry right now. Would you take a walk with me?" He extended one hand to her.

She slipped her smaller hand into his larger one without hesitation.

"Collin, you and Alice mind watching Sara for a minute?" he called out.

He only had eyes for Evangeline and was thankful his brother replied, "Love to." Collin said something else under his breath and Owen and August snickered.

Leo didn't care.

He had Evangeline by his side.

They slipped away, out into the darkness. The moon was just coming up over the eastern horizon, half-full and bright against the velvet sky sparkling with stars.

"Alice said Coop's been better," Evangeline said.

He shook his head. Sighed. "He's made promises before. Broken plenty of them. I love him but—he's a mess."

Leo had taken Owen's words to heart. He did still love his brother, but he was angry. Angry about what had happened back in New Jersey, angry that the cover up had been necessary, that Alice had been forced out of the only home she'd ever known.

There was tension in the air when Leo and Coop were in camp together—which didn't happen often. Coop had gotten himself assigned to first watch most nights, which meant Leo was asleep by the time he returned.

Leo sighed. "I don't expect he's really changed. He's just biding his time. He needs to get right with his Maker."

She squeezed his hand and boy, there was something about having her near that comforted him.

They'd walked far enough that the campfires they'd left behind had faded into the dark. The moon and stars were their only illumination now.

He stopped walking and tugged on her hand, bringing them face to face.

"I'd rather not talk about Coop any more," he said. He'd wasted enough time worrying about his brother.

Silence stretched between them. His hands were shaking with anticipation and nerves. He hoped she couldn't feel it.

He opened his mouth. "I'm sorry for walking away from you—"

"I think we should get married—" She spoke at the same time he did.

Her statement had him slack-jawed from shock.

"Maybe you should go first," she said.

His heart was pounding for a whole other reason now. "Not a chance."

When she hesitated, he prompted her. "You changed your mind about me?"

The moon limned her face silver, and he absolutely loved the stubborn tilt of her chin. "I did not. I always thought you were an exceptional man. After what happened back in Boston, I didn't think I would be able to love anyone again. But Alice set me straight on that."

His pulse raced even faster. She hadn't said she loved him, but it sure sounded like that's what she meant.

He couldn't help himself. She took a deep breath as if she was going to speak again, but he covered her lips with his. She responded to his kiss with an open warmth that made his heart sing.

She thought he was exceptional.

He broke the kiss, breathless. "My turn." He took a half

step back. He wanted nothing more than to keep kissing her, but he needed to say this. He held both her hands in his. "I am truly sorry that I walked away from you. I let my pride and my hurt feelings get in the way when I should've been there because you needed me. The truth is, it didn't take me long to fall in love with you."

She inhaled one quick breath. Hadn't she guessed? She had to have known based on the way he'd kissed her.

"Being with you and Sara is an adventure every day. It is," he said firmly when she started to shake her head. "You're not a burden to be borne, and neither is she. The way she sees the world is something special. It's a reminder I need every day." He took a deep breath and tugged her closer. His hands rested at her waist while hers came to his shoulders.

"I know I walked away once, so maybe it's going to take some time to earn your trust again. That's okay with me. I want to stand by your side. Help you start over and build your mill—your father's legacy—in the valley. You've got my promise. I'm never going to walk away again. I love you."

She was blinking back tears now and looking at him like she didn't quite believe this was happening. "I love you, too, Leo."

He felt her words settle deep inside him and joy over-flowed. He brushed a kiss on her cheek, reveling in the moment. Knowing things would never be the same. When he lifted one hand to cup her face, she rose up on tiptoe to meet his kiss.

For this moment, everything was right in the world. She loved him.

When he squeezed her waist and leaned back a few moments later, he couldn't help but grin. "You really want to marry me?"

"More than anything. Is there a preacher on the wagon train? Or can Hollis marry us?"

She wanted to marry him. Soon.

There was only one blemish on this perfect moment.

"You deserve a ring or something. It'll be a while—maybe years before I can afford something like that."

She shook her head. "I don't need a ring. You don't have to prove anything to me. Just love me."

Didn't she know? That was the easy part.

Twenty-Five

"YOU BEEN DOIN' all right?" Collin asked Maddie Fairfax.

The two of them walked side-by-side. He'd come straight from riding herd on the cattle and his horse walked behind the two of them, the reins in Collin's left hand keeping them tethered.

"I'm fine."

She didn't look fine. She looked bone-weary, with fine lines fanning away from her eyes and a stiffness to her gait that spoke to exhaustion.

Dusk was gathering around them and Hollis still hadn't called a halt for the day. The wagons rolled along, some of them creaking and groaning, not far away. Collin had found Maddie and asked her to walk with him, like they'd planned days ago.

The mood in camp had been somber since Philip had been hanged for his crimes. Or maybe it was Collin himself, and not the entire wagon train, that had been changed somehow.

He'd known what could happen on a journey like this. Natural disasters, sickness, accidents.

He hadn't expected death to come so violently.

He shook the morose thoughts away.

Why was Hollis pushing them so hard today?

Maybe the wagon master was worried that they'd faced too many delays early in the journey. Collin'd heard talk of what could happen if they met snow in the mountains.

It was easier to think about what lay ahead than recent events, but Collin realized he wasn't being very good company.

"Is your aunt any better?" he asked politely.

Irene had grown ill again. She was on bed rest in the wagon.

"I expect she'll be much recovered in a few days," Maddie said quietly.

She had her arms inside her shawl, the whole thing wrapped around her, hiding her upper body from view. Collin hadn't thought it was that cool this evening.

"Was it much warmer back home? You're from Ireland, right?" He thought someone had said that's where the family originated from. He could hear it in the lilting accent whenever Maddie spoke.

Maddie's lips pinched slightly. "It's not warm in Ireland.

She barely looked at him when she spoke, and he couldn't help noticing she hadn't really answered his question. Collin didn't know whether she was incredibly shy or just didn't like him much.

He knew he couldn't keep up this ruse. He'd only asked her to come walking with him in the first place to give him opportunity to spy on her family.

But he was done with that. Leo had found happiness with Evangeline. Collin was glad for his brother, really he was. Leo and Evangeline were going to get hitched the next time the wagon train stopped long enough to have a Sunday service.

But things had changed for Collin.

After everything that had happened the past few days, he

didn't care about the secrets of the Fairfax family. He was more interested in keeping his family safe. Including Coop.

He'd only come walking tonight to let Maddie down easy.

But with the standoffish way she was acting, maybe he should be letting her know that he wasn't going to bother her anymore.

Steven would be happy about that.

Maddie's brother was riding his massive stallion close by their family wagon that Louis was driving. When they'd begun walking, Collin had slowed their steps so they'd fallen a bit behind the wagon and fanned out to one side. He and Maddie were close enough for the overprotective Steven to keep an eye on them but far enough for a little privacy.

In fact, Steven had twisted in the saddle and was watching them right now.

Collin was going to let it go. He was. It shouldn't matter that something about Steven bugged him.

But he couldn't seem to look away.

A dog barked. Steven's horse danced beneath him. The young man struggled for control, tightening his grip on the reins.

It didn't work.

A loud *bang!* rang out from somewhere nearby. Not a gunshot, but nearly as loud.

Collin jumped.

And Steven lost control of the horse completely. The stallion reared. Steven dropped the reins. He clung to the saddle and somehow stayed on the horse.

But then the horse bolted, heading out into the open prairie, away from the wagon train.

Collin reacted without a thought, swinging into his own saddle.

That horse was too big, too spirited for Steven. The young man was going to get himself killed.

But not if Collin could help it.

Maddie called out something behind him, but he didn't

even look back as he urged his horse into a gallop. Collin's gelding wasn't as big as Steven's horse, but he was fast and liked being given his head.

They raced after Steven, flying over the uneven ground.

The stallion was wild. Maybe he'd realized he was in control, that Steven didn't have the reins and couldn't do anything to stop him. He shook his head as he ran, trying to dislodge his rider without stopping to buck.

Somehow, Steven stayed on.

If he fell now, with the horse at an outright canter, he'd break his neck. Collin could only hope to get close enough to grab the reins. Or even to grab the man from the back of the horse.

They'd already raced far enough away that the wagon train was out of sight when Collin glanced over his shoulder. He'd hoped that maybe someone else had seen, that someone might come to help.

But the plains behind him were an empty stretch of prairie grass.

When he looked forward again, he saw Steven's hat fly off his head.

There was a flash of blond hair and then the stallion took a flying leap over what might be a small washout ahead—Collin didn't have a chance to see.

Because Steven tumbled off the horse's back.

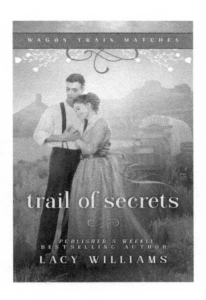

Stella is the oldest of three sisters and she's got a long history of being the one to protect and provide for her family. When a dangerous threat sent the Fairfax sisters on a wagon train journey west, Stella knew her best bet was to disguise herself as a man to keep herself and her sisters safe.

Collin Mason has secrets of his own. And his family isn't short on drama either, not with his troublemaking twin and an older brother about to get hitched. But he's the only one who sees the real Stella—and that she needs help.

Collin sees the vulnerability Stella tries so hard to hide. When he becomes the only one she can trust and she discovers that danger has followed her family, Stella must rely on him despite her reluctance...

Read TRAIL OF SECRETS

Acknowledgments

With grateful thanks to my friend Benita Jackson for being an early reader of this book and reminding me where it needed a sprinkling of passion.

Thank you to my author pals Misty, Robin, Sharon, Hallee, and Susie May. Your input for this book and the series has been so appreciated!

Also a humongous thank you to my proofreaders Lillian, MaryEllen, and Shelley for helping me clean up all the little errors.

Want to connect online? Here's where you can find me:

GET NEW RELEASE ALERTS

Follow me on Amazon
Follow me on Bookbub
Follow me on Goodreads

CONNECT ON THE WEB

www.lacywilliams.net
lacy@lacywilliams.net

SOCIAL MEDIA

Also by Lacy Williams

WIND RIVER HEARTS SERIES (HISTORICAL ROMANCE)

Marrying Miss Marshal

Counterfeit Cowboy

Cowboy Pride

The Homesteader's Sweetheart

Courted by a Cowboy

Roping the Wrangler

Return of the Cowboy Doctor

The Wrangler's Inconvenient Wife

A Cowboy for Christmas

Her Convenient Cowboy

Her Cowboy Deputy

Catching the Cowgirl

The Cowboy's Honor

Winning the Schoolmarm

The Wrangler's Ready-Made Family

Christmas Homecoming

SUTTER'S HOLLOW SERIES (CONTEMPORARY ROMANCE)

His Small-Town Girl

Secondhand Cowboy

The Cowgirl Next Door

COWBOY FAIRYTALES SERIES (CONTEMPORARY FAIRYTALE ROMANCE)

Once Upon a Cowboy

Cowboy Charming

The Toad Prince

The Beastly Princess

The Lost Princess

Kissing Kelsey

Courting Carrie

Stealing Sarah

Keeping Kayla

Melting Megan

The Other Princess

The Prince's Matchmaker

HOMETOWN SWEETHEARTS SERIES (CONTEMPORARY ROMANCE)

Kissed by a Cowboy

Love Letters from Cowboy

Mistletoe Cowboy

The Bull Rider

The Brother

The Prodigal

Cowgirl for Keeps

Jingle Bell Cowgirl

Heart of a Cowgirl

3 Days with a Cowboy

Prodigal Cowgirl

Soldier Under the Mistletoe

The Nanny's Christmas Wish

The Rancher's Unexpected Gift

Someone Old

Someone New

Someone Borrowed

Someone Blue (newsletter subscribers only)

Ten Dates

Next Door Santa

Always a Bridesmaid

Love Lessons

NOT IN A SERIES

Wagon Train Sweetheart (historical romance)